mental_floss

SCATTER
BRAINED

Also from **mental**_floss:

mental_floss *presents: Condensed Knowledge*

mental_floss *presents: Forbidden Knowledge*

mental_floss *presents: Instant Knowledge*

mental_floss: *Cocktail Party Cheat Sheets*

mental_floss: *What's the Difference?*

mental_floss: *The Genius Instruction Manual*

mental_floss

SCATTER BRAINED

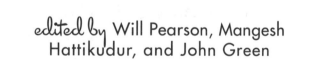

edited by Will Pearson, Mangesh Hattikudur, and John Green

written by Ransom Riggs, Will Hickman, and Hank Green

Collins

An Imprint of HarperCollins*Publishers*

HarperCollins books may be purchased for educational, business, or sales promotional use. For information, please write: Special Markets Department, HarperCollins Publishers, 10 East 53rd Street, New York, NY 10022.

FIRST EDITION

Designed by Emily Cavett Taff

Library of Congress Cataloging-in-Publication Data has been applied for.

ISBN-10: 0-06-088250-6
ISBN-13: 978-0-06-088250-1

06 07 08 09 10 WBC/RRD 10 9 8 7 6 5 4 3 2 1

CONTENTS

CONTENTS

INTRODUCTION

We at **mental_***floss* have this friend. We'll call him John, partly to protect his identity, and partly because that's his name. We like John. We always have. He's smart and funny and geekily enthusiastic about things like quantum mechanics and underrated mid-80s art rock bands. But John has one particular flaw that we all find absolutely unbearable: No matter what we're talking about, John can always connect the topic of conversation to his ex-girlfriend Maggie, who dumped him a couple years ago. Some examples:

Mangesh: "Did you know there's an actual disease called break-dancer's thumb? I mean, isn't that freaking amazing?"
John: "Remember that break-dancing movie *Breakin' 2: Electric Boogaloo*?"
Mangesh: "Yeah."
John: "It starred Ice-T. Maggie got me to start drinking sweet iced tea. She's from the South, you know."
Mangesh: "Oh. My. God. How do you *do* that?"

✖ ✖ ✖

Neely: "I just found out that if you add all the numbers of the roulette wheel together, 1–36, they equal 666."
John: "The mark of the beast!"
Neely: "I know. Crazy, right?"
John: "You know, 666 is believed to be a reference to Nero,

and Nero is a perfect anagram of Reno, the city where Maggie dumped me."

Neely: "It's been two years, dude. You gotta let it go."

It's a fascinating talent, to be sure. But no one ever thought much of it until one day a while back when we were brainstorming ideas for books. Jokingly, someone said, "We could have John write a book about the connections between his ex-girlfriend and Teddy Roosevelt."

This book, you'll be pleased to learn, is not about that connection.* But we figured, hey, if John can connect everything to Maggie, perhaps it's possible to connect everything to everything else. Perhaps we could build a single chain, hundreds of pages long, wherein each topic is connected in some strange and unexpected way to the next.

And so we did. With the help of talented writers, expert fact-checkers, and a few tortured transitions, each subject, from kissing to kung fu, leads to the next. We like to think of *Scatterbrained* as one of those eight-foot-long submarine sandwiches, except ours has Knowledge as the meat and Dumb Jokes as the main condiment.

We hope you enjoy the book—but in a way, our main objective has already been achieved: When he realized the interconnectedness of *all* knowledge while working on this book, John finally saw the silliness of his endless Maggie references. He is now living happily ever after with a woman named Janet, who—he'll be happy to inform you—was Phi Beta Kappa at Harvard (just like Teddy Roosevelt) and whose favorite novel is Stendhal's *The Red and the Black* (the colors of a roulette wheel).

---

* Although if you're interested, the connection is that they both practiced judo.

1

from
GREECE [THE COUNTRY]

UNPLEASANT EXECUTION METHODS

TOILET FACTS

BACKWATERS OF LINGUISTICS

to
GREASE [THE LUBRICANT]

TOBACCO TIMELINE

FUNERAL RITES

LATIN YOU SHOULD KNOW

LITERARY ECCENTRICS

to
GREASE [THE MUSICAL]
AND OTHER TALES FROM BROADWAY

01 Greece (the Country):
The Only Facts You Need to Know

Everyone knows the story of the marathon: Some Greek guy ran for about 20 miles from the city of Marathon to neighboring Athens, whereupon he gasped, *"Nike,"* and promptly died. (That wasn't an early form of product placement, just the Greek word for "victory.") You might not know, however, that at the first modern Olympics in 1896, the marathon distance was set at 24.85 miles (40 kilometers). So why is it 26.2 today? To please the King of England, of course! For the 1908 Olympics in London, the distance was lengthened to 26 miles so the course could go from Windsor Castle to White City Stadium and then lengthened another 385 yards so the race could finish right in front of Kind Edward VII's stadium box. Now you know whose name to curse when staggering those last miserable marathon steps.

✖ ✖ ✖

The first winner of the modern Olympic marathon, incidentally, was a Greek. Spyridon Louis, a postal worker (who trained, we imagine, by running away from ferocious dogs). He finished in 2:58:50.

✖ ✖ ✖

And you thought 99 bottles of beer on the wall was bad: The Greek national anthem, with its 158 stanzas, is the longest national anthem in the world.

✖ ✖ ✖

If you've ever found yourself legs akimbo, feet in stirrups, wondering why they call it a "Pap" smear: Greek-American George Papanicolaou created the test, which has helped reduce cervical cancer fatality rates by almost 50 percent since its introduction in the 1940s. (For some reason, "Papanicolaou smear" never caught on.)

Eat, Drink, and Be Merry

EAT . . .

Scholars believe ambrosia, the food of the Greek gods, was a purified kind of honey. It was said to give the gods strength (and if eaten by regular folk, it could even bring immortality). Also, it never caused heartburn, which is more than can be said for moussaka, the ubiquitous ground meat and eggplant casserole popular with contemporary Greeks.

DRINK . . .

The Greek gods washed down ambrosia with nectar, the aromatic wine of the Greek divinities. But palates aren't as sophisticated as they once were: These days, Greeks often mix white wine and Coca-Cola ("a poor man's Red Bull and vodka," we'll call it). So how old do you have to be to guzzle this makeshift bit of deliciousness? Just sixteen, in Greece.

AND BE MERRY . . .

To-GA! To-GA! The hedonistic toga party was invented by frat-boy Greeks, not people-living-in-Greece Greeks. In fact, ancient

Greeks wore himations, a direct ancestor of the Roman toga. But as it turns out most toga party "togas" look a lot more like himations than togas. The toga was semicircular, whereas himations, like the bed sheets generally used these days, were rectangular. But a himation party wouldn't be quite so much fun: Plato claimed that a gentleman should never extend his arm outside his himation, making both groping and beer-guzzling difficult.

FOR TOMORROW YOU DIE

Although the Roman persecution of early Christians tends to get all the attention, Christians weren't that much better when they assumed power. Greeks who continued to worship their pantheon of gods were frequently put to death until the beliefs died out in the late first millennium CE. A popular means of execution was dismemberment in public. But if you think that sounds bad . . .

02 Means to an End:

Unpleasant Execution Methods Throughout History (In Reverse Order of Preference!)

LING CHI: A slow, excruciating death, implemented a millennium ago by China's Song dynasty, *ling chi* (or "slicing") entails a piecemeal disassembling of the arms and legs by knife, culminating in decapitation. On the upside, luckier victims got to indulge in a good bit of opium beforehand, as an act of mercy. We'd argue that a better act of mercy would be not to carve up living people, but that's just us. The good news is *ling chi* was abolished. The bad news is that it wasn't until 1905, only 900 years late.

✖ ✖ ✖

SAWING: Employed by historical free spirits like Caligula, Spanish Inquisitors, and—whaddya know—the ancient

Chinese, death by sawing is kind of like the horror franchise *Saw*, except more horrific and not a movie. The convicted was strung up by the feet and sawed in twain, beginning at the crotch; his upside-down position ensured a continuous flow of blood (or whatever blood remained) to the brain, so he barely had to miss a moment of the terror until it was over. Recipients included such heinous criminals as adulterers and sodomites, plus a few saints, maybe the prophet Isaiah, and any young woman thought to be carrying Satan in her womb. That's the thing about the Beelzebaby—you never can be too sure, so kudos to the Spanish, because during the entire Inquisition, Satan's spawn wasn't born even once.

Ling chi's slower, less palatable brother, "death by a thousand cuts," appears to be an exaggeration perpetuated by traveling Westerners, apparently concerned that tales of *ling chi* weren't sufficiently disturbing.

✳ ✳ ✳

BOILING ALIVE: Fairly self-explanatory. Historically, execution by boiling is far more widespread than you'd think. In fact, it was prevalent in the Roman Empire, ancient China, Egypt, throughout the Middle East (where to conserve water they used oil), classical Japan, 17th-century India, England under Henry VIII, and Uganda under Idi Amin in the 1970s. More recently, the gruesome act seemed relegated exclusively to members of the crustacean family— until an autopsy report emerged from Uzbekistan in 2002 implicating the practice in *at least* one political prisoner's demise.

✳ ✳ ✳

BURNING AT THE STAKE: Particularly effective in the elimination of witches, heretics, Christians, Zoroastrians,

Nordic thugs, British traitors (females only, please), homosexuals, and anyone else whose flesh is not flame-retardant, burning at the stake is the straightforward but reliable, the Toyota Corolla of capital punishment. Its advantages are obvious: It's easy to do—all you need is a stake and some burning—and it makes for a flashy public-service message. The upside of death by fire: You may die of carbon dioxide poisoning before you're engulfed by flame. The downside: You might not. Given the choice, we'd rather go like '30s movie star Lupe Vélez, who committed suicide in 1944 by overdosing on sleeping pills and then reportedly drowning in her toilet. . . .

If death by fire were 40,000 shares of stock and we were your broker, we'd probably advise you to "sell." Most places either abolished it (like England, in 1790), redesigned it (America's electric chair), or never used it in the first place (Islamic law forbids it).

03 Toilet Facts

Toilets are like oxygen or boyfriends: You tend not to think much about them until the moment you can't find any. Maybe it's time to give your W.C. a little R-E-S-P-E-C-T. After all, you probably don't notice but you pay respect to the porcelain god six to eight times per day, on average—or thirty to forty times per day, if you're a six-year-old on a road trip (just joshing, kids). That makes for 2,500 trips to Flushville per year, comprising an average of three full years of your life. That's enough time to get a law degree . . . if only you hadn't spent it reading ***mental**_floss*.

Lies Your Toilet Told You

One of the best-known bits of trivia regarding the loo is that flushing one in the United States produces a clockwise swirl, whereas Australia's toilets flush counterclockwise—a phenomenon said to be driven by the contrasting effects of the earth's rotation upon the Northern versus the Southern Hemispheres. What's particularly fascinating about this oft-mentioned factoid, though, is that it's entirely false. Although grounded in a true natural phenomenon known as the Coriolis effect, this nugget of misinformation fudges the fact that over an area as small as a toilet—or, for that matter, an Olympic swimming pool—the Coriolis effect's effect is negligible. Whether in New Zealand or New Hampshire, your toilet will only flush in the direction its water jets tell it to.

✳ ✳ ✳

Nazi war criminal and Gestapo founder Hermann Göring despised toilet paper (seriously). He refused to use it and instead bought handkerchiefs in bulk.

✳ ✳ ✳

In 1993, an Argentinian prankster switched the "Women's" and "Men's" signs in a series of public toilets. We don't see why this is particularly clever—the gender divide is the same whether you all go to Room A or Room B (except that women will get to peek at some urinals). Apparently, the Argentine government wasn't impressed by it either: They sentenced the bathroom bandit to three years in the clink (which supposedly left him flushed).

✳ ✳ ✳

The separate stall, a welcome innovation if ever there was one, is a relatively modern concept. The Romans and Greeks, for instance, saw toilet time as a social occasion and sat down in groups at their open-air toilets. That brings us back to the Greeks, which brings us to . . .

04 It's All Greek to Us:
The Backwaters of Linguisics

There are a lot of languages (9,500 not counting the dead ones, by some estimates), and some people would argue that you ought to learn a couple—like, say, Spanish or Mandarin—that already have a loyal following. But why not invent your own language, coerce millions into using it, and conquer new linguistic frontiers? In case you're looking for inspiration . . .

KLINGON

Why It's Worth Learning: It's the surest way to a Trekkie's heart.

Why It Was Invented: Because *Star Trek* is so unbelievably realistic and authentic, except for the traveling-faster-than-the-speed-of-light-being-completely-impossible part.

How Long It Takes to Learn: You won't be fluent until you've memorized the surprisingly lengthy *Klingon Dictionary*.

The Basics: Of the handful of constructed languages inspired by *Star Trek*, Klingon is by far the most widely spoken. Some estimates indicate that there are thousands of Klingon speakers on Earth and billions more in the solar system. As for the language's earthly origins, however, you can thank Marc Okrand. Mr. Okrand created Klingon for Paramount Studios' *Star Trek III: The Search for Spock,* and what resulted certainly wasn't pretty. Mainly because Klingon's guttural and forceful tones reflect the warrior spirit of the Klingon people. For instance, there's no way of saying "Hello," in Klingon; the only greeting is "nuqneH' " which more or less means "Whaddya want?"

LEETSPEAK

Why It's Worth Learning: You desperately want to fit in with all the kids on AOL Instant Messenger.

Why It Was Invented: B/c ppl R layz.

How Long It Will Take to Learn: Thirty 57X, if you pay attention.

The Basics: If you've ever hung out in a chat room, you've probably seen text like "d00d r u CuTie," which certain communities of chatters believe is a) a sentence, and b) a question, even though it c) lacks punctuation, and d) contains more grammatical and spelling errors than it does letters. While the d00ds of the online world probably don't know it, such short-cut-laden, purposely misspelled typing (including "teh" for "the") is actually a typeset dialect known as leetspeak (or, more commonly, 133+5p33K). And while words like *d00d* aren't particularly hard to decode, hardcore leetspeakers can fashion sentences like: 73]-[|)0|\||<=j 15 4|\| 45$ (hints: j = y, and |< = k, and = = e).

ELVISH

Why It's Worth Learning: If elves ever show up in the world, and if they're really as hot as Liv Tyler and Orlando Bloom, you'll want to be able to talk to them.

Why It Was Invented: J.R.R. Tolkien thought that designing languages was fun.

How Long It Will Take to Learn: Years, if you want to be able to read or speak Elvish. But you can learn how to say, "Liv Tyler, you are so beautiful. Please come home with me," in just a few minutes.

The Basics: J.R.R. Tolkien actually developed several

languages during his life. Aside from a few Elvish poems in the *Lord of the Rings* trilogy, Tolkien wrote in his constructed languages mostly for his own, um, entertainment. Many of his Elvish writings since have been translated by a dedicated group of Tolkienians who go by the name Elvish Linguistic Fellowship (ELF—so clever, those Tolkien fanatics). The Quenya dialect of Elvish (as heard in the movies) sounds a lot like Finnish, but most of the vocabulary came straight from Tolkien's mind. And yes, Tyler really *is* speaking Elvish in the movies, although many Tolkienians claim her accent is, like, totally bogus.

ESPERANTO

Why It's Worth Learning: So you can help rebuild the Tower of Babel.

Why It Was Invented: To end all disagreement, war, strife, and unhappiness.

How Long It Takes to Learn: Esperanto advocates say it's easier to learn than most any other language. But still, that means you will only be able to say "Pierre is going to the library with his friend the acrobat" for the first six months.

The Basics: Between 1877 and 1885, a Polish Jew named L. L. Zamenhof constructed a language. He hoped that a universal, easy-to-learn language might create a world where people could communicate with one another using words rather than bullets. His language, Esperanto (which means "one who is hoping" in Esperanto and "one whose hope is a bit unrealistic" in English), caught fire with European intellectuals, but never took root with the public at large. Today there are some two million Esperanto speakers worldwide, but on the whole, people still prefer communicating with bullets: In the 20th century, there were some 110,000,000 war-related deaths.

MIRROR ENGLISH

Why It's Worth Learning: It's not.

Why It Was Invented: Someone held a book up to a mirror and said, "Hey. I can't read that."

How Long It Takes to Learn: If you own a mirror, you're basically already fluent.

The Basics: In mirror English the letters are reversed, so as to be read in front of a mirror, and the meaning of the words is also reversed, so as to seem clever. For example, if you wanted to say, "Your little friend, Boris, sleeps with the fishes," you might write "Boris, is awake with the birds. Your big enemy," Or take the first sentence of the following quotation we just made up: "I will never understand the concept of 'dry hair.' You don't need a special *shampoo* to de-dry your hair. You need *water*." That first sentence might become "You will soon understand the concept of 'greasy hair.'"

05 Hair Grease
(and Other Major Greases)

Hair grease is a substance called sebum (a term also used to refer to body oil generally) that is secreted by the sebaceous glands onto hair follicles. Sebum isn't really bad for you, but it does contain some cholesterol, which means it's probably not ideal to eat.

✖ ✖ ✖

How fast is faster than greased lightning? While it's difficult to say how much greasing would increase its speed, regular lightning is pretty darn fast: Lightning can travel as fast as 93,000 miles per second, about half the speed of light. And just so you know: Your chance of getting hit by lightning is about 1 in 600,000. If you play Powerball (1 in 120,526,770), you may not like the odds, but take comfort: Only 20 percent of lightning-related injuries are fatal.

✖ ✖ ✖

Sure, Bo (Jackson) knew baseball and football, and "Neon" Deion Sanders had a flashier nickname. But no two-sport star showed quite the talent for multitasking as Earle "Greasy" Neale, who played pro baseball and football *and* coached a college football team—all at the same time. Greasy won a World Series in 1919 with the Reds (acknowledged, the ignominious "Black Sox" let the Reds win, but

Fat Boy Grim

So you just got dumped, and you want to eat a Classic Triple Cheeseburger from Wendy's (963 calories). And since what's-her-name isn't around to chastise you for being a fat boar, you eat *two* of them (50 grams of saturated fat, or 250 percent of your suggested daily allowance). So why are you so hungry for fatty food? Well, because it's yummy. Also, given your depressed state, you need an influx of happy hormones, and in lieu of antidepressant medications, greasy grub will work in a pinch. The human body absorbs fatty foods more slowly than proteins or carbohydrates, which makes us feel full longer. And so long as the body feels full, it releases hormones communicating contentment. Nicotine, incidentally, releases similar hormones, which is part of the reason it's said to be an appetite suppressant. In short, you don't need love so long as you have Classic Triple Cheeseburgers. Or . . . cigarettes (not that we're endorsing either!).

with Greasy on their side, the Reds might have pulled it out regardless) and two NFL championships as coach of the Philadelphia Eagles.

✖ ✖ ✖

Sure, the butter flavoring in microwave popcorn is rich in greasy goodness. But extended exposure to it seems to cause a fatal and irreversible lung disease. The disease commonly known as "popcorn packers' lung" brings to mind black lung, another occupation-related respiratory disease. Speaking of *lung*-winded words, *pneumonoultramicroscopicsilicovolcanoconiosis* is famous to lexicographers for being the longest word in the 2nd edition of *The Oxford English Dictionary*. It is defined as "a factitious word alleged to mean 'a lung disease caused by the inhalation of very fine silica dust' but occurring chiefly as an instance of a very long word."

05 Tobacco Through the Ages
A Timeline

1492: Columbus, having sailed the ocean blue, notices Indians smoking and thus becomes the first known European to encounter tobacco. Indians take pains to look "cool" while smoking so as to exact a small measure of revenge for their coming annihilation.

1556: The fashion-forward French become the first Europeans to take to smoking.

1577: By now, European doctors are recommending smoking to combat bad breath and cancer. That's right: bad breath and cancer.

1604: King James I publishes a scathing indictment of smoking, calling it a "vile custom" and a "filthy novelty" that is "dangerous to the lungs." Tobacco company executives promptly swear before the king's court that there is absolutely no proof that smoking is vile, filthy, a custom, or a novelty, let alone dangerous to the lungs.

1610: Sir Francis Bacon notes that it is kind of hard to quit smoking.

We're just going to skip ahead here 384 years to:

1994: Seven tobacco executives swear before the United States Congress that nicotine is not addictive.

Now, back to our timeline:

1624: Pope Urban VIII threatens to excommunicate those who snort snuff because sneezing is too similar to orgasm. (Really.)

1724: Pope Benedict XIII, a smoker, overturns Urban's ban on tobacco.

1761: British scientist John Hill publishes the first study to point out that ever since people started snorting snuff, there seems to be a lot of nose cancer floating around.

1776: American tobacco is used as collateral for French loans, helping to pay for the American Revolution.

1890: Per capita, American adults chew three pounds of tobacco annually.

1912: Dr. Isaac Adler publishes research that, for the first time, argues strongly that smoking may cause lung cancer. Tobacco company executives race to Dr. Adler's house and swear on a stack of Bibles that smoking does no such thing.

1921: Tobacco marketing has kicked into high gear: R. J.

Reynolds spends $8 million on advertising, promoting their slogan "I'd Walk a Mile for a Camel" (And, Boy, Would I Be Out of Breath).

1940: Per capita, American adults smoke 2,558 cigarettes per year (more than seven per day).

1950: Three major studies definitively prove that smoking causes lung cancer.

1963: After trying out a tattooed sailor, Philip Morris settles on a cowboy as the Marlboro Man. Beginning in 1975, the Marlboro Man is played by Wayne McLaren, who dies in 1992 at the age of 51 from lung cancer.

1966: First Surgeon General's Warnings appear on cigarette packages in the United States.

1971: TV and radio tobacco ads for cigarettes disappear as a result of 1969 legislation.

2004: Despite extensive antismoking efforts, tobacco smoke still kills about 440,000 Americans every year. Leading us to . . .

07 Funeral Rites Around the World

IRAQ: Did cavemen invent the funeral? That was the question posed in the 1950s, when the excavation of nine Neanderthals in northern Iraq's Shanidar cave produced evidence that the 60,000-year-old stiffs had been left there together, perhaps as part of a concerted effort to mourn their passing. American anthropologist Ralph Solecki, who led the dig, cited a layer of many types of seeds and pollen found surrounding one grave as proof that prehistoric man invented not only the funeral, but also the floral arrangement. Many remain unconvinced by Solecki's findings, however—and barring the excavation of a receipt from the Grogg & Grogg Bereavement Hut, the mystery of Shanidar will never be solved.

✖ ✖ ✖

INDIA: Think traditional funeral services are for the birds? Then do your best to die somewhere in the vicinity of one of the Towers of Silence, where one of the neighborhood's Zoroastrians might give you a chance to have the exciting air burial you've always dreamed of. Per their religion, Zoroastrians leave their dead atop a local tower, where vultures handle the nasty business of disposing of the spiritually impure flesh. From there, it's as simple as throwing the bare bones down into the tower's pit, where they can rest for all eternity (in a pile with all the others). And while the Zoroastrians do offer several convenient locations thoughout the deserts of Bombay and Iran for disposing of remains, you should probably act fast. Remember, the recently declining populations of vultures make this a limited-time-only offer, so don't delay.

✖ ✖ ✖

GHANA: If you want an ornate but relatively inexpensive coffin, you'll be well advised to avoid the American funeral home racket altogether and die, as no less an American than W.E.B. Du Bois did, in Ghana. There, the dead are often buried in elaborate "fantasy coffins" that come carved in everything from airplane to fish styles.

✖ ✖ ✖

SWEDEN: The latest technology in funeral services is that of Swedish marine biologist Susanne Wiigh-Masak, who in 1999 patented the "ecological funeral," a meticulous cryotechnological process that does all the work of decomposition so that you won't have to. The process begins with the reduction of the corpse to a fine powder that makes your dead self healthier for the environment. Next, scientists extract the leftover metals and send them off to be recycled—meaning that in your next life part of you may just be a Volkswagen Beetle. Finally, the remains are ready to be sent back into Earth—and you can be sure that Earth will be glad to have you, thanks to your biodegradable casket.

✹ ✹ ✹

ROMAN EMPIRE: When an ancient Roman was dying, the oldest surviving male of the family leaned in close to the dying person and attempted to inhale the dying breath (that's just . . . not sanitary). They did try and put the fun back in funeral, though. The rites lasted several days and often featured hired mourners and professional dancers. And while most people know that the Romans liked a party, not many are aware of how much they liked fire. Almost all Romans were cremated, and their ashes placed in a *columbarium*— which is just one of many Latin words worth knowing. . . .

⬛ Latin You Should Know

Why do you need these Latin phrases? Well, like Latin teachers always say, Latin lives on in plenty of English words and phrases. But mostly, it's worth learning a bit of Latin because *omnia dicta fortiori, si dicta Latina.**

Ad hoc: Literally meaning "for this," it's generally used to mean improvised.

---

* "Everything sounds more impressive when said in Latin."

Ad infinitum (not to be confused with *et cetera*): "To infinity, without end."

Caveat emptor: "Let the buyer beware."

Citius altius fortius: "Faster, higher, stronger"—the motto of the modern Olympics.

Columbarium (see previous page): A collective tomb in ancient Rome that was also used as a house for pigeons and doves.

Corpus christi: "The body of Christ."

Cuius est solum eius est usque ad coelum et ad inferos: "Whoever owns the land it is theirs up to the sky and down to the depths." The state of Kansas used this law in the 1970s to argue that airlines could not serve liquor when flying over Kansas, a dry state. "Kansas," Attorney General Vern Miller said, "goes all the way up and all the way down." (If that's true, Kansas can lay claim to, and prohibit drinking in, about 82,282 square miles of western China.)

Deus ex machina: "A god from the machine," usually referring to an awkward and contrived resolution to conflict. The phrase got its start from the plays of Euripides, in which a god was lowered down onto the stage via a mechanical crane to sort out intractable conflicts and confused plots.

Id est: "That is," often abbreviated "i.e."

In media res: "In the middle of things." Stories like *Paradise Lost* or *The Odyssey* or *Sweet Valley High* #17 begin in the middle.

Ipso facto: "By the very fact," i.e., "absolutely, regardless of circumstances."

Lupus est homo homini: "Man is a wolf to man." No one knew this better than the Romans.

Magnum opus: Great work

Nolo contendere: When you want to enter a plea of "No contest" in as fancy a way as possible.

Opus Dei: "The work of God" or "An outsized villain in a bestselling novel."

Quod erat demonstrandum: "That which was to be demonstrated." Abbreviated QED, often the end of a mathematical proof.

Sic semper tyrannis: "Thus always to tyrants," the motto of Virginia and the last thing John Wilkes Booth said before shooting Abraham Lincoln.

Sic transit gloria: "Glory fades," popularized by Max Fischer, founder, Rushmore Double-Team Dodgeball Society.

Sub poena: "Under penalty," as in "Do this or you're in trouble."

Tabula rasa: A "blank slate"—John Locke's description of the human mind without knowledge.

Veni, vidi, vici: "I came, I saw, I conquered," and the most oft-mispronounced Latin phrase in the world. It should be pronounced, WAY-nee, WEE-dee, WEE-kee.

Et ignotas animum dimittit in artes: "And he sent forth his spirit among the unknown arts." A beautiful quote from Ovid that we use out of alphabetical order because James Joyce used it in *A Portrait of the Artist as a Young Man,* and we need to move on to him. . . .

09 Literary Eccentricities,
a.k.a. Portrait of the Artist as a Lunatic

James Joyce was nearly always seen wearing an eye patch, which was *not* mere accessorizing: He suffered from glaucoma throughout adulthood and eventually went completely blind. In fact, he dictated much of his last book, *Finnegan's Wake,* to his research assistant, Samuel *Waiting for Godot* Beckett.

✖ ✖ ✖

But Joyce sometimes wore five wristwatches on one arm, which *was* mere eccentric accessorizing. He also asked his wife, Nora Barnacle, to sleep with another man so he could understand the feeling of being cuckolded, which seems a bit odd. (Nora declined.)

✖ ✖ ✖

Nineteenth-century French poet Charles-Pierre Baudelaire, who besides being quirky was addicted to opium, once famously wrote, "If you would not be the martyred slave of time, / Get drunk! . . ." He wasn't kidding about making the most of his time: In his house he kept a clock with no hands that bore the inscription "It's later than you think." Incidentally, the positively batty Baudelaire also happened to own a pet bat, which he'd captured at (where else?) a graveyard.

✖ ✖ ✖

Charles Dickens could not sleep unless his bed was aligned in a north–south position. Also, he habitually touched certain objects three times "for luck."

✖ ✖ ✖

When he was 29, George Bernard Shaw lost his virginity to a widow 15 years his senior. Apparently, it wasn't all that good, because thereafter Shaw rarely, if ever, had intimate physical relationships—not even with his wife, to whom he was married for 45 years.

✖ ✖ ✖

Although *Peter Pan* author J. M. Barrie did not like the taste of brussels sprouts (as would befit a boy who never grew up), he often ordered them at restaurants. Why? "I cannot resist ordering them. The words are so lovely to say."

✖ ✖ ✖

"Little Mermaid" and "Thumbelina" author Hans Christian Andersen was so intensely afraid of being buried alive that he left a note by his bed each night that read, "I only *appear* to be dead." Andersen was right to feel anxiety around sleeping, incidentally: In 1875, he died as a result of injuries sustained falling out of bed.

For much of his career, Graham Greene wrote 500 words a day. Exactly. No matter if he was in the middle of

✖ ✖ ✖

Although Emily Dickinson was not quite the utter recluse that she is often made out to be, she was unquestionably eccentric: She wore white from head to toe, exclusively, for the last several years of her life.

By the Numbers:
THE BOOK EDITION

4,391 words in the longest sentence of James Joyce's *Ulysses*.

1,536 pages in the *abridged* version of Samuel Richardson's *Clarissa* (1748), generally agreed to be the longest English novel.

37 bestselling books with titles beginning *Chicken Soup for the* published between 1993 and 2003.

131 books in the original Babysitters Club series.

3 years that the average novel stays in print.

2 novelizations of the musical *Grease* currently in print. . . .

10 Grease (the Musical)
and Other Tales From Broadway

First staged in an abandoned trolley barn in Chicago, *Grease* went on to become a surprise Broadway hit. With its satirical jabs at '50s teenagers and irresistibly catchy songs, the show ran for 3,388 performances (approximately equal to the number of bad movies John Travolta has since starred in). When the Broadway musical became a movie in 1978, the satire was taken seriously by some, and a brief rebirth of greaser style followed. Danny Zuko and his heartthrob, Sandy Olsson, played by Travolta and Olivia "Let's Get Physical" Newton-John, respectively, became *the* couple to emulate, and the movie grossed some $380,000,000. Four years later, *Grease 2* came out and grossed approximately $380. The sequel, which had an inferior director and unmemorable songs, was one of the bigger box office disappointments in cinematic history, and sounded the death knell for the big-budget movie musical (at least until *Moulin Rouge* and *Chicago* hit the screen).

✳ ✳ ✳

Lost in Translation

The movie *Grease* was released in Mexico with the memorable title *Vaselina,* which got us to thinking about other memorable translations. Limiting ourselves just to Bond movies:

Dr. No → Chinese: *Tie jin gang yong po shen mi dao* ("007 Seized the Secret Island")

From Russia with Love → French: *Bons baisers de Russie* ("Good Kisses from Russia")

A View to a Kill → Japanese: *Utsukusiki emono tachi* ("The Beautiful Prey")

License to Kill → Japanese: *Kesareta Licence* ("The Cancelled License")

Octopussy → Chinese again: *Tie jin gang yong po bao zha dang* ("007 Averted the Blast Plot")

Of the 39 Broadway theater houses, only six sport addresses actually *on* Broadway in New York. Most are in the theater district around Times Square. But "off-Broadway" theaters are sometimes located *on* Broadway. And that's not even to mention off-off-Broadway theaters. Wait. Who's on first?

The distinction, it turns out, has to do with the number of seats in a theater, not its location. Broadway theaters generally have more than 500 seats; off-Broadway, between 101 and 499; and off-off-Broadway, fewer than 100.

✳ ✳ ✳

One of the central figures in early Broadway history was Edwin Booth. One of the most successful actors of his day, Edwin also opened an early New York theater (which, in the great tradition of Broadway theaters, soon closed). Booth also helped establish the original Players' Club (the one for people in the arts, not the one for polyamorous pimp daddies).

✖ ✖ ✖

Incidentally, Edwin's father, Junius Booth, was one of the most famous actors of his generation as well. After Junius died, Walt Whitman wrote, "There went the most noble Roman of them all." But Walt didn't have to live with Junius, who was (like many noble Romans) a mean drunk. His sons bore much of their father's alcoholic wrath, and Edwin drank, too. And while Edwin's brother, John, did abstain from booze, he wasn't exactly a saint. Less talented than either his father or brother, John found a way to be famous nonetheless—John, of course, murdered Abraham Lincoln on Good Friday, 1865. Speaking of dead presidents . . .

2

▮▮ Dead Presidents

Ex-presidents and political rivals John Adams and Thomas Jefferson died on the same day, July 4, 1826—50 years to the day after the signing of the Declaration of Independence. Jefferson died first (after asking, "Is it the Fourth?"), but Adams was unaware of it when he mumbled his own last words a few hours later: "Thomas Jefferson still survives."

✖ ✖ ✖

Underrated president Millard Fillmore had suffered a stroke that his doctor felt would best be treated by withholding food (you know what they say—"Feed a fever, starve a stroke!"). Desperately hungry, Fillmore was finally given a spoonful of soup. "The nourishment is palatable," Fillmore noted dryly—and then died.

Dying in Office

According to the Bureau of Labor Statistics, "timber cutter" was one of the most dangerous jobs in America in 2002, with an annual fatality rate of 117.8 per 100,000 workers, or 0.12 percent. Now, we don't want to take anything away from timber cutters—partly because they tend to own chainsaws—but, technically, American president is a more dangerous job. In the 216 years the gig has existed, eight presidents have died while in office—an overall annual fatality rate of 3.7 percent.

✖ ✖ ✖

Remarkably, Ulysses S. Grant is the only American president ever to have died of cancer. Grant suffered for the last years of his life from then-untreatable throat and tongue cancer. But something about being near death did wonders for his literary talents: His presidential memoirs, which he was still revising in his final days, were published by Mark Twain and are still considered the greatest literary achievement of any president. (Jimmy Carter's picture book—see p. 158—aside.)

✖ ✖ ✖

By the Numbers

9 entirely or partly caused by stroke

7 heart disease

4 pneumonia

1 asthma (Van Buren)

1 alcoholism (Franklin Pierce)

1 cherries and milk (Really. See below.)

No U.S. president has ever died in the month of May.

✖ ✖ ✖

The morning of July 4, 1850, dawned bright and hot in Washington, and President Zachary Taylor spent the day dedicating the Washington Monument. Already over-heated, he got home and made the mistake of gorging on cherries and milk. The combination caused—well, there's no polite way to put it—diarrhea, which combined with his heat stroke proved fatal.

✖ ✖ ✖

Now and then some riddle lover will query, "Which American presidents are not buried in U.S. soil?" The two technically true answers:

1. "Bill Clinton, George W. Bush, George H.W. Bush, and Gerald Ford." They are not buried in U.S. soil because they are not dead.

2. "Adams, Quincy Adams, Garfield, and Wilson—among several others." They are not buried in U.S. soil because they are all interred in aboveground sarcophagi.

✖ ✖ ✖

William Henry Harrison's inauguration day in 1841 happened to be extraordinarily cold and wet. Harrison, wanting to appear presidential, decided to give his inaugural speech without a topcoat or a hat. That might have worked out okay, except he proceeded to give the longest inaugural address in American history, clocking in at just over one hour and 45 minutes. Shortly thereafter, Harrison developed pneumonia. He died on April 4, 1841, having been president for 31 days—and all for want of a hat. . . .

02 Great Hats
(or the Heads of Heads of State)

THE NAPOLÉON

Popularized By: Napoléon, naturally

Hat Story: Napoléon was known for his tall, folded-brim felt hats. Some hypothesize, in fact, that Napoléon is remembered as short because his gigantic hats dwarfed the rest of him.

Pluses: The last guy who wore it conquered most of Europe.

Minuses: From a distance, it looks like a giant possum is asleep atop your head.

THE BERET

Popularized By: Saddam Hussein (president, Iraq) and Max Fischer (president, Rushmore Beekeepers Club)

Hat Story: Originally worn in ancient Greece and Rome, the beret reached the Basque country by way of traders. The Romans color-coded their berets (white, for instance, could only be worn by aristocrats).

Pluses: Looks simultaneously authoritative and artsy

Minuses: Also looks French

THE FEZ

Popularized By: King Hassan II (King of Morocco in the 1960s) and Shriners

Hat Story: This visorless, flat-topped, betasseled felt cap became part of the official Turkish dress code under Sultan Mahmud II in the 1800s and remained so until being outlawed in 1925, two years after Turkey became a secular republic.

Pluses: Friends and family will be able to spot you in a crowd: "Just look for the tassel!"

Minuses: Won't keep the sun out of your eyes; people will start calling you Fezzy McTasselman.

THE BOWLER, A.K.A. THE DERBY

Popularized By: Charlie Chaplin (who played a dictator in *The Great Dictator*) and Benito Mussolini (who played a dictator in World War II)

Hat Story: Originally designed as a kind of stylish hard hat, the narrow-brimmed bowler first appeared in 1850 and for the next several decades was *the* hat for those who thought top hats too pretentious—or expensive.

Pluses: Much sexier than today's hard hats (if also less hard)

Minuses: It didn't work that well for Duckie in *Pretty in Pink*.

EGYPIAN DIADEM

Popularized By: King Tutankhamen (of Egypt) and Steve Martin (of *Saturday Night Live*)

Hat Story: Tut's royal crown, made of gold, glass, and semi-precious stones, featured a vulture and a cobra (representing goddesses of lower and upper Egypt) to protect the leader. Martin's was made of plastic.

Pluses: It's good to be king!

Minuses: Airport metal detectors

THE TOP HAT

Popularized By: Abraham Lincoln (16th president of the United States)

Hat Story: A Cantonese hatter designed the first silk top hat in China for a French dandy back in 1775—but top hats didn't catch fire until the 1820s. Honest Abe actually wore a variation on the top hat called the stovepipe hat, the hat being straight rather than wider at the top.

Pluses: Uber-retro, and black is very slimming.

Minuses: Kids always asking you to pull a rabbit out of it. Or people might mistake you for the mascot for the LeMoyne-Owen College Magicians basketball team, which is a none-too-subtle way to get us to . . .

03 Sports Mascots

☞ *"Effectiveness" is calculated on how many national championships were won by the teams with a particular class of mascot between 1995 and 2004 in the following sports: men's baseball, women's softball, men's and women's basketball, men's football, and men's hockey.*

THE ANIMALISTIC

Examples: Lions and tigers and bears—oh my! Also cougars, wildcats, bruins (which are bears), wolves, etc. Pretty much any animal capable of killing people

Atypical Examples: University of California Santa Cruz banana slug, the Upper Iowa University peacock

Advantages: Fierce, violent, mean

Disadvantages: Generally not potty trained

Effectiveness: 62 percent!

Anecdotally: The Cal State Fullerton baseball team (which won national championships in 1995 and 2004) came to be known as the "Elephants" back in the early 1960s when they staged "the first intracollegiate elephant race in human history" before 10,000 (presumably stoned) spectators.

THE RACIST

Examples: A dozen colleges still use "Indians" as mascots, and the pro team in the nation's capital still goes by the moniker "Redskins."

Atypical Example: The Florida State University Seminoles, who have explicit permission from the Seminole Nation to use "Chief Osceola" as their mascot

Advantages: Terrifying—particularly to early-19th-century settlers of the American West.

Disadvantages: Racist and uninformed

Effectiveness: 2 percent

Anecdotally: In response to the widespread apathy about Native American mascots, a group of students at the University of Northern Colorado formed "The Fighting Whities" intramural basketball team in 2001.

THE LOCALLY FLAVORED

Examples: Cornhuskers, Volunteers, Sooners, Hoosiers, Buckeyes

Atypical Example: The Stanford Cardinal (singular—they're not named for the birds but for the color)

Advantages: Wins the hearts of your fans

Disadvantages: Bragging that you can husk corn isn't intimidating.

Effectiveness: 17 percent

Anecdotally: "Sooners" refers to people who entered Oklahoma *sooner* than the Indian Appropriation Act of 1889 said they could, so—in a roundabout kind of way—it's also exploitative of Native Americans.

THE PUNNY

Examples: Frost (Texas) High School Polar Bears; Poca (W. Va.) High School Dots; Lincoln High School Abes; Gonzaga University Zags

Atypical Example: South Dakota School of Mines and Technology Hardrockers (also atypical because—they need a mascot?)

Advantages: May elicit an initial chuckle from new students

Disadvantages: Like all puns, gets old fast

Effectiveness: 0

Anecdotally: Oddly enough, Converse College was *not* paid by Converse shoes to name themselves the "All Stars." And perhaps for good reason—in 2005, the basketball team went 3–24.

Senior Superlatives

Most Likely to Have Been Thought Up by a Five-Year-Old Girl: Starkweather-Munich (N.Dak.) High School Magic Storm

Most Likely to Have Been Thought Up by a Five-Year-Old Boy: Rowland Hall (Utah) High School Winged Lions

Most Likely to Encourage Juvenile Delinquency: Yuma (Ariz.) High School Criminals (whose school once occupied an abandoned prison)

Most Nimrodish: Watersmeet (Mich.) School Nimrods

Most Likely to Bravely Mumble "Please, Sir, I'd Like Some More": Centralia (Ill.) High School Orphans

Most Indebted to a 1980s Sitcom: Blooming Prairie (Minn.) High School Awesome Blossoms

Most Likely to Gross Out Opponents: Algonac (Mich.) High School Muskrats. (The muskrat is like a regular rat, except four to five times bigger. Muskrats are also extremely close cousins to lemmings, which reminds us . . .)

04 Fourteen Lies Your Mother Told You

The Lie: Lemmings commit suicide en masse.

The Truth: Lemmings are stupid, not depressed. The myth of lemming suicide goes back a long way—at least to Freud, who in *Civilization and Its Discontents* (1929) examined the human death instinct in the context of the purported mass suicide of lemmings. But suicidal lemmings didn't fully enter the pop culture lexicon until Disney made the "documentary" *White Wilderness* in 1958. Disney shipped dozens of lemmings to Alberta, Canada (where they do not live), herded them off a cliff, filmed the poor creatures falling to their deaths, and passed it off as nonfiction. Ah, the magic of Disney. In fact, lemmings aren't suicidal. They're just dumb. When the tundra gets crowded, they seek out new land. Sometimes they fall off cliffs.

✳ ✳ ✳

The Lie: When elephants get ready to die, they go to elephant graveyards.

The Truth: When elephants are ready to die, they just fall down and do it, just like the rest of us.

✳ ✳ ✳

The Lie: Throwing rice at weddings causes birds to explode.

The Truth: Throwing rice at weddings causes birds to have something new and delicious and totally undangerous to eat. In fact, there are many species of birds in Asia who survive primarily on uncooked rice, which they take from fields. The myth had its start in a 1988 Ann Landers column in which she discouraged readers from the practice. The USA Rice Federation (motto: "Proving There Is a Federation for Everything") immediately debunked Landers's story, but, surprisingly, Ann Landers had a broader readership than the USA Rice Federation.

✷ ✷ ✷

The Lie: Chewing gum stays in your digestive system for seven years.

The Truth: Chewing gum, like anything else, stays in your digestive system for an average of about 20 hours. Like a lot of indigestible things people eat (fingernails, lettuce, Froot Loops), chewing gum gets passed through the gastrointestinal tract as roughage.

✷ ✷ ✷

The Lie: If you don't wait an hour after eating to get in the swimming pool, you will get a cramp and die.

The Truth: Exactly 0 deaths have ever been attributed to entering a pool too quickly after eating.

✷ ✷ ✷

The Lie: Walt Disney is cryogenically frozen.

The Truth: Walt Disney was the opposite of frozen. His body was cremated two days after his death in 1966.

✷ ✷ ✷

The Lie: The original Harlem Globetrotters are from Harlem.

The Truth: Not a single one was from New York. Almost all of the original Globetrotters were from Chicago, where the team was founded in 1926. They took on "New York" to seem more cosmopolitan as they toured the Midwest and changed it to "Harlem" in 1930.

✷ ✷ ✷

The Lie: Adam and Eve ruined everything for the rest of us by eating an apple.

The Truth: Adam and Eve ruined everything for the rest of us by eating an unnamed fruit. The exact wording: ". . . the fruit of the tree that is in the middle of the garden" (Genesis 3:3).

✖ ✖ ✖

The Lie: Mussolini made the trains run on time.

The Truth: When seeking to explain why masses of people will sometimes support evil regimes, you often hear folks say, "Well, Mussolini made the trains run on time." Poor example. If you're taking an indefensible position, well, Hamas *does* provide schools and medical care to Palestinians. Sri Lanka's Tamil Tigers, who conscript child soldiers and lead the world in suicide bombings, *did* give aid to Sri Lankans in the wake of the 2004 tsunami. But Mussolini never made the trains run on time. During World War I, the Italian rail system became woefully inconsistent, and it's true that by the time Mussolini took power in 1922, the trains were more punctual—but mostly because of construction work done in the years before he took power.

✖ ✖ ✖

The Lie: The Great Wall of China is the only man-made object visible from space.

The Truth: Thousands of man-made objects are visible from space. Furthermore, the Great Wall of China is not among them. To quote astronaut Jay Apt, "Although we can see things as small as airport runways, the Great Wall seems to be made largely of materials that have the same color as the surrounding soil."

✖ ✖ ✖

The Lie: Van Gogh cut off his left ear and mailed it to a prostitute.

The Truth: He only chopped off the *bottom half* of his left ear—somewhere between a Tyson–Holyfield fight and a full-fledged ear-ectomy. And he didn't mail it to a prostitute. Some claim he *gave* it to a prostitute named Rachel (hey, we never said he was well adjusted), but he never *mailed* anything. Given his complete financial distress (in his lifetime, he only sold one painting), Vincent could hardly afford the postage.

✳ ✳ ✳

The Lie: Hair grows back thicker and darker after you shave it.

The Truth: Sadly, it does not—although balding men surely wish it did. Hair may seem to grow back thicker because short hairs tend to feel and look dark and coarse, but it's an illusion. Nor does your hair keep growing after you die. Nor does 100 strokes with the brush before bedtime improve the health of your hair. Nor can any fancy-pants shampoo repair your split ends (someone had to say it).

✳ ✳ ✳

The Lie: You only use 10 percent of your brain.

The Truth: You, beloved and brilliant **mental_***floss* reader, use *all* of your brain. And so does everyone else. PET and MRI scans of the brain show that while you don't use all of your brain all the time, you use all of it some of the time. Frankly, we're offended on your behalf that anyone would *ever* say that your well-flossed, knowledge trap of a brain was only functioning at 10 percent capacity! Maybe those idiots think Van Gogh mailed his ear to a hooker, but not you! Again, even those idiots use all their brains as well, but we're on a roll here. It's just total bull! Incidentally, if you've ever wondered why we say "bull" rather than "cow" or "hog" or "three-toed possum" . . .

05 Bulls:
From Chicago to Pamplona

Watch us get through this without cursing: *Bull,* as in *baloney,* is not short for BS. Believe it or not, the Middle English word *bull,* meaning not a male cow, but "false talk or fraud," entered the lexicon about 800 years before BS did. The word *bull* is as unrelated to the animal as the word *bear* (as in "grin and bear it") is to a grizzly. Witness, for instance, the Middle English epic poem *Cursor Mundi:* "Said Christ to the hypocrites, you are all full of wickedness, treason, and bull." Although it might be more fun if Christ were telling the hypocrites they were full of . . . you know, they were actually just full of meaningless talk.

✖ ✖ ✖

If you've never heard of the Chicago Zephyrs (founded 1962) or the Chicago Stags (founded 1946), that's because they just weren't very good basketball teams. Of course, from 1966 to 1983 the Chicago Bulls weren't very good, either. But their luck changed when, in 1984, they scored the third pick of the NBA draft and picked up a 21-year-old shooting guard named Michael Jordan. Under the command of the man that Larry Bird called "God disguised as Michael Jordan," the Bulls won their first, second, third, fourth, fifth, and sixth (i.e., last) NBA championships. Since his departure (his retirement, then his move to the Washington Wizards, and then his retirement again), the Bulls have gone back to being Zephyr-esque.

✖ ✖ ✖

The animal commonly known as the bull, not to mention the cow and the ox, descended from the aurochs, a now-extinct species that lived in Europe until the 15th century.

The aurochs were such a wonderful source of meat, and so comparatively docile, that people often took them into their homes and treated them like family—that is, whenever they weren't castrating, slaughtering, or eating them.

✳ ✳ ✳

The aurochs got us back for this mistreatment, though, when the first human contracted smallpox (a mutated form of the aurochs' disease cowpox). In the ten centuries since smallpox first infected humans, more than 100 million people have been killed by the disease.

✳ ✳ ✳

Pamplona

Once a year, the city of Pamplona celebrates the return of the remains of its patron saint, San Fermin, by feasting, dancing, and running away from a half-dozen bulls stampeding through the city's streets. A dangerous activity, to be sure, but much safer if you follow the simple guidelines laid out in a brochure published in several languages by the city of Pamplona. Some direct quotes:

If you get up right in the path of the running bull, he could go through you as clean as a knife cuts through butter.

Do not stand still.

Making the run on a drunken spree is totally out of order.

If you think we'd all be better off with something safer, such as the running of, say, the penguins, take note that there *is* such a thing: the daily penguin parade in Phillip Island Nature Park off the coast of Australia. Every evening, after spending the day feeding at sea, a troupe of penguins march up a beach surrounded by spectators who've come from around the world to witness their routine. So far, there have been no fatalities, but no statistics are available on how many ice-cold Budweisers have been stolen. . . .

🎬 Commercial Mascots

Missing: The Bud Ice Penguin

Last Seen: Dooby, dooby, doo-ing

Possible Location: scouring the U.S. for someone, anyone, who still drinks Bud Ice

Warning: Penguins are slippery.

You Probably Remember: With his creepy catchphrase ("Dooby, dooby, doo") and unrelenting desire to steal Bud Ice (which, it could be argued, was an act of charity more than malice), the penguin became hugely popular. But like Budweiser's other ad campaigns, this one faded into oblivion faster than you can say *Whazzzzzzup?*

You May Not Remember: That Budweiser was sued by Munsingwear shortly after the Bud Ice penguin became a star, arguing that Budweiser's campaign amounted to slander of penguin advertising mascots everywhere.

✖ ✖ ✖

Missing: The Noid

Last Seen: 1992

Possible Location: Wherever there are pizzas to be ruined, you'll find the Noid.

Warning: May be armed with Noid Bombs or the magic Noid Wand

You Probably Remember: The claymation embodiment of evil, the Noid sought to bring down the Domino's Pizza empire in the 1980s and early '90s by destroying pizzas in clever ways. Inevitably thwarted by heroic pizza deliverypeople, Domino's advertised itself as the pizza place where you could be sure to "avoid the Noid." The Noid became so popular that he even inspired the Nintendo game Yo!Noid.

You May Not Remember: Enraged by the maligning of the Noid name, a Georgian named Kenneth Lamar Noid held two Domino's employees hostage for five hours in 1989, which in the end only lent further credence to the notion that it's best to avoid Noids.

✱ ✱ ✱

Missing: Esky

Last Seen: gracing the front cover of *Esquire*

Possible Location: retirement home in Palm Beach

Warning: May be old, but he's still plenty frisky.

You May Remember: *Esquire*'s big-eyed, bigger-mustachioed mascot from the magazine's inception in 1933 finally retired in 2003. What Esky lacked in cartoon looks, however, he must have made up in personality, as he was constantly doted on by the fairer sex. During World War II, for instance, Esky cavorted with women from Paris to Polynesia. From the '50s onward, the magazine relied on Esky less and less, until his face became a mere dot in *Esquire*'s i. By 1980, Esky had disappeared from most covers entirely (who needs a dirty old cartoon man when you can have Burt Reynolds?).

You May Not Remember: Esky peeking into Elizabeth Taylor's cleavage in the April 1952 issue of *Esquire*.

✖ ✖ ✖

Missing: The Puttermans

Last Seen: Indefatigably hawking Duracell batteries in the '90s

Possible Location: Might be hiding out with the little girl from *Small Wonder*

Warning: May be rechargeable—don't let them highjack* your outlets.

You Probably Remember: Duracell used the robotic Putterman family to respond to the enormously popular Energizer bunny ads. The logic seemed to be "Sure, those Energizers can power a dumb little *bunny,* but Duracells can fuel an entire robot family." But apparently the Putterman ad campaign wasn't running on Duracells: While the Energizer bunny is still going and going, the Puttermans puttered out quite a while back.

You May Not Remember: the secret of the Putterman crying game: Grandma was played by a man.

07 Scrabble

In the depths of the Great Depression, an out-of-work architect named Alfred Butts decided to pass the time by designing a board game that integrated his passions for crossword puzzles and anagrams. Butts read the *New York Times* to gauge the commonness of various letters (though he later admitted that his game includes too many *I*'s) and assigned each of them a point value. The game, then called Lexico, was basically finished in

---

* Yes, *highjack* is a legitimate alternate spelling of *hijack.* It's also the highest-scoring SCRABBLE-able word in this story (28 points!) and takes us nicely to our next topic. . . .

Bingo!

The holy grail of Scrabble players is the bingo—using all seven tiles on a single play gets you 50 points and respect from even the best players. The highest scoring bingo you're likely to ever see in Scrabble is the 81-point *quizzify* (the second *Z* would be a blank). But Scrabble nerds have figured out a massively hypothetical and contrived situation wherein the word *oxyphenbutazone* could be played for a stunning 1,778 points.

1933. But it didn't take off until 1949 (by then, Lexico had become Scrabble), when the president of Macy's department store played it, loved it, and ordered it for his store just in time for Christmas.

✻ ✻ ✻

On December 15, 1979, Canadian newspaper reporters Scott Abbott and Chris Haney were playing a game of Scrabble when they decided to create a game of their own: Trivial Pursuit. That's right. "All-American Edition" aside, Trivial Pursuit is the work of Canadians! (Of course, if you want to buy American, allow us to discreetly plug **mental** _floss: The Trivia Game.)

✻ ✻ ✻

One of the world's best professional Scrabble players is former National and World Champion "GI" Joel Sherman. Sherman earned his nickname not because of his militaristic playing style but because his gastrointestinal tract often gives him trouble during stressful matches.

✻ ✻ ✻

The word *scrabble* (meaning: to grope frantically) is playable in Scrabble.

The Shorties

The first step for any serious Scrabble player is to learn the playable two- and three-letter words. We don't have the space to get into the 977 three-letter words, but knowing the 96 two-lettereds will help you play more words (and make more points) at a time and get rid of spare tiles at the end of a game—and impress your friends. Some examples:

Do, re, mi and all their friends make the cut. So does *ut*, which was once widely sung as the first note in the scale. *Do* replaced it in the early 20th century.

Et, surprisingly enough, is a legitimate past-tense form of *eat.*
   Sample usage: "Er, I et it." (*Er* is also playable.)
In ancient Egyptian cosmology, the *ba* is the eternal soul.
   Sample usage: "You want me to sell my ba? Nah."
In the 19th century, Baron Carl von Reichenbach coined the word *od* to refer to the force that pervades the universe—which he believed was particularly manifested in magnets and crystals. Why *od*? The baron's own answer: "Everyone will admit it to be desirable that a unisyllabic word beginning with a vowel should be selected." Well, jeez, if *everyone* will admit it, then by all means.
   Sample usage: "Every time I remember that Baron von Reichenbach made up a word that got in the dictionary and I haven't, I feel the od within me deplete."

And the entire list (not that we're getting paid by the word or anything): *aa, ab, ad, ae, ag, ah, ai, al, am, an, ar, as, at, aw, ax, ay, ba, be, bi, bo, by, de, do, ed, ef, eh, el, em, en, er, es, et, ex, fa, go, ha, he, hi, hm, ho, id, if, in, is, it, jo, ka, la, li, lo, ma, me, mi, mm, mo, mu, my, na, ne, no, nu, od, oe, of, oh, om, on, op, or, os, ow, ox, oy, pa, pe, pi, re, sh, si, so, ta, ti, to, uh, um, un, up, us, ut, we, wo, xi, xu, ya, ye, yo.* Eight of those 96, incidentally, make an appearance in the Dr. Seuss classic *Green Eggs and Ham.* . . .

08 One Fish, Two Fish:
The Life and Times of Dr. Seuss

In 1960, publisher Bennett Cerf bet Dr. Seuss $50 that Seuss couldn't write a book using only 50 different words. So Seuss wrote *Green Eggs and Ham*, which became an instant picture book classic. Cerf apparently never paid up, incidentally. *Green Eggs and Ham* marked the apex of Seuss's minimalist-vocabulary period, and it was an awfully impressive feat (we used 50 different words just to tell you about it).

✖ ✖ ✖

When *Dr. Seuss Goes to War*, a collection of Geisel's World War II–era cartoons created for *PM* magazine, was published in 1999, the American public was stunned. How could the author of peace-loving, Truffula Tree–hugging children's books have penned wartime cartoons that attacked Japanese Americans and depicted the Japanese as bucktoothed buffoons? Some argued that Seuss was only

Seuss: The Basics

Theodor Seuss Geisel wasn't actually a doctor (at least not until his alma mater, Dartmouth, gave him an honorary PhD), but his unique poetic meter and kid-friendly, leap-off-the-page illustrations made him one of the most successful children's writers in history (220 million books sold). From books intended to teach vocabulary and reading skills (like *The Cat in the Hat*) to allegorical tales of power-hungry turtles and environmental destruction (*Yertle the Turtle* and *The Lorax,* respectively), Dr. Seuss was a vital innovator in the world of children's books for more than fifty years. When he arrived on the kid-lit scene, children's books were boring, lifeless tomes (once you've seen Spot run a couple times, you're ready to give up reading for good). Dr. Seuss created picture books that we *wanted* to read.

reflecting his times; others argued that racism is racism (regardless of whether it's in a box or with a fox).

✖ ✖ ✖

Before he started speaking for the trees, Dr. Seuss was, well, a sellout. For fifteen years he wrote and designed ads for the corporate monolith Standard Oil. In a series of ads hawking Standard's pesticide Flit, Geisel coined the popular catchphrase, "Quick, Henry, the Flit!" which was sort of the "Mikey likes it!" of its time.

✖ ✖ ✖

While it would probably be a slight exaggeration to say that Dr. Seuss singlehandedly ended the Cold War, *The Butter Battle Book* was one of

Horton Spies a Kegger

Dr. Seuss came from a long line of German brewmasters, which perhaps explains how he came to throw a drunken bash during his Dartmouth days. Due to school policy (and also federal law, since Prohibition forbade drinking in those days), Ted's excellent venture got him fired from his position at *The Dartmouth Jack-O-Lantern,* the college's humor magazine. But the wily Geisel never let The Man keep him down: He kept writing for the *Jack-O-Lantern,* adopting the pseudonym "Seuss" (his middle name) to get by the censors.

the most influential anti-arms-race books of the '80s. Telling the story of the absurd war between the Yooks and the Zooks (whose sole disagreement is whether one ought to eat bread butter side up or butter side down), Seuss subtly challenged the Reagan administration's emphasis on defense over social welfare programs. For six months, the book was on the *New York Times* Best Sellers list—for adults. Every single one of Seuss's books sold well to kids, of course—not that these kids coming up next would ever deign to read him. . . .

09 We Can't All Be Mozart:
Lesser Child Prodigies

THE TOTAL FAILURE

The most accomplished child prodigy in American history was probably William James Sidis (1898–1944). With an IQ estimated to have been 250–300, Lil' Will read the *New York Times* at 18 months old, passed the entrance exam to MIT at age eight, and learned scores of languages before he hit puberty. (Sidis's parents, needless to say, pushed him a little.) When Sidis graduated from Harvard at 16, he was at the pinnacle of his career. For most of his adult life, he lived alone and worked as a bookkeeper. His main hobby was writing books about extraordinarily obscure subjects. For example,

The Success-But-in-a-Bad-Way

Psychologist Lewis Terman (1877–1956), one of the men responsible for the modern IQ test, began the largest-ever study of highly gifted children in the 1920s. Terman and his colleagues followed young Californians with IQs above 140 for their entire lives. Surprisingly, almost none of Terman's subjects made a significant impact in any academic or artistic field. The one exception, however, was George Hodel, who made an impact in the field of serial killing. Hodel most likely killed a bunch of women in the 1940s and '50s—including the actress Elizabeth Short, known as the Black Dahlia. Hodel was smart enough to evade capture in his lifetime, but in a plot twist so good it seems contrived, Hodel's son, Steve, who became a homicide detective, ended up discovering his father was probably behind California's most famous unsolved murder.

he wrote one about streetcar transfers, which his own biographer called "the most boring book ever written."

THE NEVER-GOT-A-CHANCE

By the time Josef Hassid (1923–1950) turned 12 he was being hailed as the greatest violinist in centuries. Over the next few years he made nine recordings, which are as valuable to violin aficionados as great bootlegs are to Deadheads. Sadly, Hassid developed schizophrenia in his late teens. Even more sadly, he happened to develop schizophrenia at the height of Europe's psychosurgery craze. He died from a botched lobotomy at the age of 26.

THE UNDERAPPRECIATED

Maria Gaetana Agnesi (1718–1799) wrote the 18th century's most influential book on differential calculus *and* integral calculus (which sounds like a very impressive accomplishment, even if we don't understand it), and she was only the second woman in European history to be appointed a full professorship in mathematics. Plus, she delivered an hour-long speech—in Latin—on the subject of women's rights to education. When she was *nine*. And yet today, hardly anyone's ever heard of her.

BEATING THE ODDS

The son of an extremely demanding father, Norbert Weiner (1894–1964) entered college at 11 and received his PhD in mathematics from Harvard when he was 18. But his transition from successful prodigy to successful grown-up was fraught with depression, anger, and general immaturity. He eventually persevered and ended up inventing the field of cybernetics, the study of abstract systems and controls. (Weiner used cybernetics to make American artillery fire more accurate.) Despite his eventual success, Weiner had mixed feelings about his upbringing. Surprisingly enough, it wasn't easy to grow up smart and named Norbert. Talk about a kid who needed kung fu lessons. . . .

10 Sweep the Leg, Johnny:
A History of Fighting and Defense

JUDO

Created by: Jigoro Kano, (1860–1938)

History: Jujitsu, meaning (curiously enough) "the gentle practice," was the catchall name for deadly Japanese unarmed combat. Jigoro Kano removed the deadliest moves and called it judo, "the gentle way."

Perfected by: Probably no one you know. Of 50 medal winners in the 2004 Olympics, only one (American Jimmy Pedro, Bronze) speaks English as a first language.

Advantages: Judo uses the opponent's weight and power to their disadvantage, which makes it tough to fight little girls.

Best Moves: The crucifix submission hold, which sounds at once sacreligious and pervy, is so powerful you can break your opponent's neck.

KUNG FU

Created by: The Chinese, circa 500 BCE

History: Kung fu is a collective term for Chinese martial arts. Encompassing many styles of combat, kung fu has a long and intricate history that culminated in a bunch of B movies.

Perfected by: Bruce Lee (not David Carradine or Keanu Reeves)

Advantages: You've got a broad range of techniques at your disposal, from drunken boxing to tai chi. If you know all of kung fu, there are few butts you probably cannot kick.

Best Moves: Although it sounds funny, drunken boxing is perhaps the most deadly and difficult kung fu style.

Best Defense: If you've just made Jackie Chan angry, your best bet is probably a plane ticket.

BOXING

Created by: Homo sapiens, circa 4000 BCE

History: The earliest written record of boxing is from ancient Greece, but there is evidence of boxing matches more than 6,000 years ago. Boxing was probably the first martial art, the first self-defense technique, and the first sport.

Perfected by: The only undefeated heavyweight champion was Rocky Marciano (49–0).

Advantages: One good punch is all you need.

Best Moves: The force of an uppercut comes not only from the arm and shoulders, but also from the legs and hips—making it the most powerful punch in boxing.

Best Defense: Probably a gun. Even if you can't block their punches, they'll have a hard time blocking your bullets.

MORTAL KOMBAT FOR SEGA GENESIS

Created by: Midway Home Entertainment, Inc., 1992

History: The Street Fighter arcade games captured quarters of millions of preteens. Mortal Kombat logically extended that genre by making it gorier.

Perfected by: Teenage boys

Advantages: You can tell your mom it increases hand–eye coordination.

Best Moves: "Fatality"

Best Defense: B B B B B B!

MIDDLE SCHOOL BULLIES

Created by: Poor self-esteem

History: For about as long as adults have been hitting each other, so have children.

Perfected by: Our nemesis, Aaron Bishop, was awfully good at it.

Advantages: Pathetic opponents can be selected from a huge population of weaklings.

Best Moves: Gut punches cause discomfort but leave little evidence of wrongdoing.

Best Defense: In our experience (and we've got plenty), hiding your math textbook underneath your denim jacket can bruise a bully's knuckles. Failing that, one can always hire a tenth grader. But to do that, you've got to learn a thing or two about money. . . .

II Dead Pre$idents:
Historical Tidbits About American Currency

Paul Revere did not in fact shout that the redcoats were coming, but he did design the very first paper money in America, a 12-pence note for the Massachusetts Bay Colony in 1776.

It's Easy to Be a Millionaire

If you ever feel like making change for a penny, it'll be nice to know that one American penny can be divided into 10 mills. Gas prices, for instance, are expressed in mills $2.789, and five mills (a ha'penny) is still given to an old man in a Christmas carol. If that doesn't ring a bell, you may recognize mills from their sinister roles in *Superman III* and *Office Space*. Mills now have so little value that it would cost more than one mill to print the words *one mill* on a dime-sized piece of paper.

✳ ✳ ✳

While Revere was busy designing notes based on British pence, the rest of the country was already forsaking the British monetary system in favor of the Spanish (hence our current use of dollars rather than pounds). Spanish dollars were called pieces of eight because they were often stamped into eight bits that could then be used for making change. Hence two bits of a Spanish dollar equaled a quarter. Now you know why we chant "two bits, four bits, six bits, a dollar" to generations of bewildered children.

✳ ✳ ✳

But the Spanish dollar's story does not end there. Chronic American laziness had its affects on the word *peso*, which began to be abbreviated "PS." As Americans got still lazier the two letters began to lie on top of one another. When, finally, we reached the peak of our laziness, the hump of the *P* disappeared into the curve of the *S* and we were left with $.

✖ ✖ ✖

The largest number of U.S. dollars owned by any one entity is the property not of Bill Gates, but of the United States government, which has borrowed over two trillion dollars from itself. If you're confused, you probably should be. When the United States runs out of money, we just ask for the money from the treasury and give them an IOU (Treasury bill). The treasury then prints the money and gives it to the government to use.

The Cost of Money

If you've ever wondered how much a dollar is really worth, it costs the U.S. mint around six cents to print each of the 37 million bills it prints per year. The mint saves some money by making sure that old bills, when practicable, get recycled—and that brings us to environmentalism. . . .

3

01 Sittin' in a Tree:
Environmental Activism New and Old

HEEEEERE'S RACHEL

So, how did Rachel Carson, a modest civil servant by day, become *the* rock star of the conservation movement and a modern hero to greenies everywhere? By publishing a little book called *Silent Spring,* of course! In 1962, Ms. Carson's tome unleashed the forces of global environmentalism as we know it. Focusing on the effects of now-infamous pesticides like DDT on fish and birds (like killing them—hence a *silent* spring), the book basically elucidated the nasty repercussions pesticides could cause through the food chain. DDT was banned by the newly formed EPA in 1972, but not without some controversy: Critics argue that banning one of the most effective pesticides known to man has allowed malaria-carrying flies to flourish.

WHEN GREEN GETS MEAN

In 1999 alone, there were more than 1,200 fire bombings and acts of vandalism in Britain attributed to animal rights activism. (Compare that to just 313 such acts in the U.S. between 1979 and 1993.) These included a midnight raid on a mink

Puking for America
(A.K.A. ONE "RALPH" YOU'D NEVER VOTE FOR!)

Forget capping smokestacks and dumping dead fish in corporate offices (credit Chicago's own environmental crusader Jim "the Fox" Phillips for those innovations). The award for most creative act of civil disobedience goes to Earth First! who invented the "puke-in." All you need is some green cottage cheese, a little ipecac, and a roomful of unsuspecting strangers. Earth First!'s (we're worried they'll stage a puke-in if we leave out their exclamation point) favorite targets have been shopping malls at peak Christmas season, where they "puke" to protest any- and everything from old-growth logging to genetically modified foods.

farm that released thousands of would-be fur coats into the English countryside and a nasty letter-writing campaign that sent razor blades dipped in rat poison to animal lab researchers.

THE NONPROFIT PROPHET

Zoroaster wasn't the only religion-founding prophet to advocate environmental sustainability—Muhammad mandated *khalifa*, or stewardship over nature, but he was probably the first. Zoroastrians see themselves as the caretakers of the Seven Creations (sky, water, earth, plants, animals, humans, and fire) and are so concerned with the purity of nature that they are forbidden from entering rivers for fear of polluting the water.

THIS LAND WAS YOUR LAND, THIS LAND IS NATIONAL PARK LAND

Ole Teddy Roosevelt is often viewed as the grandfather of the American conservation movement. In his two terms, he set

aside more federal land for national parks and nature pre-
serves than all his predecessors combined—more than 230
million acres altogether. But before you pronounce him Saint
Teddy the Preserver, check the stats of his 1909 African sa-
fari: His hunting party bagged more than 5,000 animals,
among them some of the last remaining white rhino. Had
T.R. actually been interested in becoming a saint, however,
he surely would've benefited from . . .

02 How to Become a Catholic Saint:
A Step-By-Step Guide

The process of canonization was developed in the 10th century by Pope John XV after the Vatican decided that determining sainthood by public opinion, which had been the
practice up until that time, left too much room for error. Back
then, you just needed to be immensely popular. Now, it's a
little more complicated:

1. You need to die. (Sorry, no exceptions.) Generally, the
   process of canonization cannot begin until five years
   after death—although after Mother Teresa died,
   groups advocating her canonization convinced the
   Vatican to relax the rule. Still, talk about hurry up and
   wait: The process itself typically takes between 10 and
   100 years.

2. A local bishop will investigate your virtues. If and when
   sufficient virtue is uncovered, the bishop will name you
   a Servant of God and send his information on to the
   Vatican for further review.

3. A gaggle of theologians and cardinals called the Congregation for the Causes of Saints, under the guidance of a postulator—finally, a use for that B.A. in philosophy—evaluate your life, and if they like what they see, they pass the buck yet again, this time to the pope.

4. The pope will then proclaim you venerable, meaning that you are now officially a role model of Catholic virtue. One nifty perk: Venerable-ness entitles you to have Catholic prayer cards printed in your likeness, which encourage the faithful to pray for a posthumous miracle to be wrought by your intercession. (Incidentally, we're willing to trade you a Mother Teresa rookie card for a Saint Christopher MVP.)

5. The next step is beatification, and the solution to this one is multiple choice. To become beatified, the venerable must either:

    a. have been martyred. Generally, martyrdom is your A-1 ticket to sainthood (10,000 martyrs were once beatified in a single ceremony), but the thing about martyrdom is that it generally hurts (see, for instance, Saint Apollonia, who had her teeth pulled one by one by the Romans).

    b. have been responsible for at least one miracle during your lifetime. Mother Teresa, for instance, was beatified when the Congregation for the Cause of Saints verified that a woman in India had her cancer cured by pressing a picture of Teresa against herself.

6. Once beatified, you'll earn the title "blessed," and then you must be credited with at least one posthumous

miracle before you can be canonized and become an official Catholic saint.

7. Wait, there's more? Don't forget about specializing! As a "patron saint," of course. If you've been canonized and have some special proclivity or talent on your résumé, you could be named a special protector or guardian of a particular illness, occupation, church, country, or cause. The aforementioned Apollonia, for instance, is the patron saint of toothaches. And Saint Isidore of Seville, who reputedly wrote the first encyclopedia, is in hot contention to become the patron saint of the Internet. Which also makes him a potential patron for geeks in general, including . . .

03 Band Geeks

Name: Trent "Nine Inch Nails" Reznor

Geek Level: ★★★   Well, his best friend is Marilyn Manson. That's *some* people's definition of cool.

Long before he began making the angriest and scariest music in the world, Trent Reznor may have been the world's biggest high school band geek. He played tuba in the jazz band, sax in the marching band, and, as if searching for that trifecta of perfect geekhood, was in the drama club to boot. His breakout role? He was voted "best in drama" by classmates for playing Judas in *Jesus Christ Superstar.*

✳ ✳ ✳

Name: John Coltrane

Geek Level: 0 stars   Extremely, extremely low.

Only John Coltrane could make being in the high school band cool. After learning to read music from local pastor and scoutmaster Warren Steele, Coltrane joined the dance band at William Penn High School in High Point, North Carolina. He started out on clarinet but, fortunately for the entire world (and all of music to come), eventually switched to saxophone.

✳ ✳ ✳

Name: Bill Clinton

Geek Level: ★★   He's the geek we always wanted to be: the one who gets the girls.

Arguably the most famous of former band geeks, U.S. president emeritus Bill Clinton was the top saxophone player in his high school band. He practiced daily, attended band camp every summer, and won first chair in the Arkansas state band's sax section. We can only conclude that either Arkansas' state band had a terrible sax section or Clinton's talents had atrophied somewhat by the time he played sax on *The Arsenio Hall Show* in 1992.

✳ ✳ ✳

Name: Frank Zappa

Geek Level: ★★★★   He named one of his own children Dweezil, after all.

Frank Zappa played drums in his school marching band until he was thrown out for smoking in uniform. Zappa went on to compose, arrange, and conduct an avant-garde performance piece for the student orchestra. Show-off!

✳ ✳ ✳

Name: Drew Carey

Geek Level: ★★★★

Carey played cornet and trumpet in the marching band. He's come a long way since his geeky band days, forging a career for himself as, well, a geeky comic.

✹ ✹ ✹

Name: GG Allin

Geek Level: At some point, Allin crossed over from geek to freak. He gets the full ★★★★ for freakiness.

Before dropping out of high school, Allin played drums in the band. He went on to become one of the most notorious frontmen in punk-rock, jailed more than 50 times for onstage antics ranging from defecating on his audiences to fighting brutally with fellow band members. Allin's legal name, incidentally, was Jesus Christ Allin—GG was a nickname that we cannot begin to explain in print. But speaking of nicknames...

04 Just Plain Terrible:
How Bad Monarchs Earned Their Monikers

IVAN THE TERRIBLE (1530–1584)

Ivan IV was Russia's first and possibly its most terrible tsar—embroiling his empire in disastrous wars with Sweden and Poland—but it wasn't questionable foreign policy that earned him his catchy nickname. Exceedingly paranoid after first wife, Anastasia, was poisoned in 1553, Ivan began killing almost indiscriminately. In addition to bludgeoning his own son to death and drowning an entire village of 1,500 in an icy river, Ivan is best known for blinding the architects of St. Basil's Cathedral in Moscow after its completion: He was

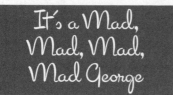

It's a Mad, Mad, Mad, Mad George

Few royals have ever had a more appropriate nickname than England's George III (1738–1820), a.k.a. George the Mad. For much of his later life, the monarch American colonists loved to hate battled insanity brought on by a rare blood disease called porphyria. Of course, scientists now suspect that the medication George was given to "control" his madness probably didn't help, particularly because it contained arsenic. And however patriotic you may be, it's hard to hate a guy who was so many cards shy of a full deck. In fact, in his final years, George was walking around insisting that he could communicate with angels and trees (none of which were advising him to pull out of America, apparently).

so impressed with its design, he wanted to make sure they never again built anything as beautiful.

VLAD THE IMPALER (1431–1476)

Also known as Dracula and widely known as the historical inspiration for Bram Stoker's novel *Dracula*, Vlad III of Walachia didn't do much actual blood drinking. Rather, the Romanian prince's nickname was inspired by his favorite method of execution: impaling people on pikes, sticks, and other sharp things. While his nasty rep was exaggerated somewhat by German pamphleteers bent on his defamation (for which their newfangled printing press came in handy), there is certainly some truth to the legends. On one occasion, Vlad is said to have invited beggars to a feast at his castle and then burned it to the ground, thus eliminating poverty in his kingdom.

YAZDEGERD THE WICKED (?–420)

Like any historical figure, Old Yazdegerd's level of atrociousness varies depending on whom you talk to. While ruling the Sassanian kingdom of Persia from 399 to 420 CE he clashed with the Zoroastrian priesthood, who dubbed him "wicked." His name literally meant "made by God," PR gold that just didn't stick.

Sticks and Stones May Break My Bones

Not every monarch was blessed with a fearsome "the Terrible" or an awe-inspiring "the Magnificent." Some royal nicknames are just plain weird, like 10th-century English King Ethelred the Unready (circa 978–1016): His nickname is a pun on his real name, Unraed, which in Anglo-Saxon means "indecisive." Louis V of France didn't achieve much in the one year he was king (986–987) so he was dubbed Louis the Sluggard. Some names need no explanation: Fortún of Pamplona, the One-Eyed; Eirik II of Norway, the Priest Hater; Louis II of France, the Stammerer. Lest we forget, monarchial nicknaming isn't just an historical phenomenon; contemporary Duchess of York Sarah Ferguson's (Fergie's) battle with obesity earned her the title "Duchess of Pork" in British tabloids. She's made the most of her rep, however, publishing self-help guides like *Dieting with the Duchess* as well as a kiss-and-tell-all, *My Story*. Of course, that brings us to our story on kissing and telling. . . .

05 K-I-S-S-I-N-G:
Tidbits from the History of Kissing

No one really knows where the first smooch came from. One less-than-romantic theory suggests it began with ancient mothers passing chewed-up food to babies, which is 1) not sexy, and 2) gross. And kissing isn't universal: People in Japan and Siberia only started kissing relatively recently, and some sub-Saharan African societies still don't do it.

✖ ✖ ✖

Perpetual Morning Breath

The erotic significance of the kiss didn't become dominant in Europe until the 17th century. Not coincidentally, that was around the same time that dentists in France first promoted the use of toothbrushes. (Yes, the French were on the cutting edge of dental hygiene!) Before toothbrushes, the average European mouth was such a grim place that 16th-century maids often carried clove-studded apples when courting, insisting their suitors take a bite before attempting a kiss.

A thousand years ago, ceremonial kisses were much more common than today. There was the holy kiss of peace, exchanged to symbolize unity in Christ; the kiss of veneration, bestowed on holy objects; you even got a kiss when you received an academic degree. By the 18th century, however, much of that ceremonial pecking had been replaced by handshakes, oaths, and written documents. One ritual kiss is still as popular as ever: that of couples sealing their marriage vows.

✖ ✖ ✖

German psychology professor Onur Güntürkün spent

two years watching people make out in public parks and airports, eventually observing 124 "scientifically valid" kisses. He concluded that people are twice as likely to tilt their heads to the right when kissing than to the left. What's the deal? Turns out our kissing proclivities are determined way in advance of the junior prom: According to Güntürkün, the direction you turn your head while in the womb will likely be the direction you tilt your head when kissing.

✖ ✖ ✖

Kissing has been banned repeatedly. Roman emperor Tiberius outlawed kissing in public ceremonies, hoping it would help curb the spread of herpes. In 16th-century Naples kissing was punishable by death, and in 1439 Henry VI banned it to combat the plague. In 2004, Indonesia passed laws that ban not only public nudity, erotic dancing, and "sex parties," but also punish public kissing with up to five years in prison. Flashing carries a stiff penalty, too:

Behind the Kiss: FAMOUS SILVER SCREEN SMOOCHES REVEALED

GONE WITH THE WIND

While it's probably the most famous kiss in movie history—Rhett kisses Scarlett fiercely, then carries her, protesting, up a grand staircase to bed—Vivien Leigh's ability to keep it together was astounding. According to Hollywood insiders, Clark Gable's halitosis on the set was so bad, Leigh didn't want to kiss him at all!

YOU'RE IN THE ARMY NOW

Not to be confused with the 1994 Pauly Shore film of similar name, this 1941 flick holds the record for the longest unbroken kiss in Hollywood history. So, how long is almost too long for Hollywood? Jane Wyman and Regis Toomey locked lips for a good three minutes and five seconds.

> **KISS**
>
> At 48 minutes, Andy Warhol's experimental film is easily the longest picture about kissing: It consists of one static shot, twelve real-life couples, four minutes each. And while Warhol's weird, obsessive focus is almost unwatchable, we're still waiting for his sequel, *Second Base*.

"I see London, I see France . . . ," but if Indonesian police see your underpants, you could be fined up to $25,000. Speaking of which . . .

06 A Very "Brief" Secret History of Underwear

1323 BCE: Egypt's King Tut is entombed alongside a wealth of jewelry, furniture, lamps, jars—and 145 loincloths. He's also entombed with over 400 statues of servants meant to clean said undies, just in case heaven doesn't have washing machines.

634 CE: The loincloth begins to fall out of fashion in Europe. It's replaced by looser-fitting braies, which are basically cloth hose for men. Luckily, they come with easy-access openings at the crotch for convenience—if not modesty.

1390: Geoffrey Chaucer kvetches about the tunic's scandalous rise to midthigh level (for which undergarments neglect to compensate) in "The Parson's Tale" of *The Canterbury Tales*: "Alas! Some of them show the very boss of their penis and the horrible pushed-out testicles that look like the malady of hernia in the wrapping of their hose; and the buttocks of such persons look like the hinder parts of a she-ape in the full of the moon."

1482: King Edward IV forbids persons below the rank of Lord to expose their genitals with short tunics, sparking an outcry among fashion-forward Englishmen. They respond by inventing the codpiece, a simple piece of cloth covering their naughty bits.

1525: Henry VIII—perhaps insecure about his inability to produce a male heir—stuffs his codpiece, starting a trend that transforms its formerly flat, utilitarian shape into a conspicuous bulge, then an exaggerated, protruding loaf.

1793: The cotton gin is invented, simultaneously increasing demand for slave labor and cotton underwear, which could now be mass-produced. The union suit, an early version of long johns, became the standard 19th-century undergarment. Rural men often wore the same union suit all winter, washing it only when spring arrived.

19TH CENTURY: Scholars speculate that one of the reasons women constantly faint in Victorian novels is that Victorian women really *did* constantly faint—because uber-tight corsets so restricted their lung capacity.

1880: Rear today, gone tomorrow: The bustle, a padded frame that enhances the shape of a woman's derrière, reaches the height of its popularity after 200 years of on-and-off use. Ten years later it disappears entirely.

1909: Horace Greeley Johnson invents the Kenosha Klosed-Krotch union suit, essentially long johns as we know them today. For his contribution, he was dubbed "the Edison of Underwear."

1919: Women's enthusiasm for athletic pursuits like bicycling and tennis make restrictive corsets impractical; trouserlike "bloomers" become popular instead.

1922: Perhaps the most important year in the history of

women's underwear (at least from a man's perspective): a luxurious new kind of underwear with pleated chiffon, crepe, and satin is popularized by flappers. It comes to be called "lingerie" (for the French for "underwear").

1970: The thong begins to appear on Brazilian beaches. Apparently, underwear fashion has come full circle, returning to the days of loincloth-wearing, butt-baring simplicity. Appropriately, however, *thong* is actually an ancient word, derived from the Old English *thwong*, meaning "flexible leather cord." Which means that—had he been so inclined—Shakespeare might have penned Sisqo's tune as "Thwong Song." Which brings us to the Bard himself (no, not Sisqo). . . .

07 Will the Real Will Shakespeare Please Stand Up?

Shakespeare's true identity has been the subject of intense academic debate and bizarre conspiracy theories since the 18th century. While most of the conspiracy claims have been debunked and almost all scholars believe the historical William Shakespeare wrote the plays attributed to him, the rumors persist. So who was Shakespeare if Shakespeare wasn't Shakespeare? Here are the usual—and a couple of the more unusual—suspects.

FRANCIS BACON (1561–1626)

Bacon was a philosopher, essayist, and politician whose brilliant mind and humanist bent seem to fit Shakespeare's work like a glove. Turn-of-the-century cryptographers latched onto the word *honorificabilitudinitatibus*, found in act 5, scene 1 of *Love's Labour's Lost*, as evidence. By rearranging its many letters, they spelled *hi ludi, F. Baconis nati, tuiti orbi*, a Latin anagram that translates to "these plays, F. Bacon's offspring, are preserved for the world." Later cryptographers, however, also found anagrams "proving" authorship by Dante Alighieri and Babe Ruth.

EDWARD DE VERE, 17TH EARL OF OXFORD (1550–1604)

Edward's proponents point out similarities between Shakespeare's plays and de Vere's biography (the latter's father-in-law, Lord Burghley, is thought to be the model for *Hamlet*'s Polonius). Unique turns of phrase appear in both Shakespeare's work and Edward's letters, and passages

Christopher Marlowe: A MAN WALKS INTO A BARD

OK, let's get this straight: Marlovians propose that, facing the death penalty for heresy, Marlowe faked his 1593 death in a bar fight, adopted the pseudonym "William Shakespeare," then penned the Bard's legendary canon. While the dates do match up nicely—Shakespeare's first play, *Venus and Adonis,* was published in 1594—the fact that no famous person is known to have ever successfully faked his or her death reminds one of Occam's Razor: "Given two equally predictive theories, choose the simpler." Dying in a bar fight? Much simpler.

underlined in de Vere's Bible show up throughout Shakespeare's plays. Compelling as this seems, however, de Vere died too soon, in 1604; Shakespeare still had 11 plays to write.

QUEEN ELIZABETH I (1533–1603)

Old Liz loved her theater and poetry, so she was a big patron of both. In fact, she even penned a couple of sonnets. But does that make her Shakespeare? A handful of scholars argue that it might and point to similarities between famous portraits of the Bard and the queen as evidence, suggesting that Shakespeare's likeness was based upon the "real" author of his work. Alas, the fact that she spent most of her time defeating the Spanish Armada and colonizing America seems to leave the lady's hands free of any ink spots.

KING JAMES I OF ENGLAND (1566–1625)

Malcom X perpetuated this theory, mentioning it in his *Autobiography*. James commissioned his famous English translation of the Bible by asking the best poets and scholars of the day to help out. Fifty-four did, but only 51 of them are known. X suspected that Shakespeare (a.k.a. James) was one of the three mystery writers. Here's the "evidence": The Bard was 46 when the King James Bible was completed. In its translation of the Book of Psalms, the 46th word in the 46th Psalm is "shake," and counting backward from the end, the 47th word is "spear." Shaky proof, certainly, but without absolute *dis*proof. Of course, some folks will believe anything: that aliens landed at Roswell, say, or that eating a tiger penis enhances the sex drive. . . .

08 Strange Aphrodisiacs
(a.k.a. Really Lovin' Spoonfuls)

If this is what it takes to make a special someone fall for you, we're not sure it's worth it! Balut is a Filipino delicacy so off-putting to Westerners that eating it was a challenge on *Survivor: Palau*. Literally an aborted duck fetus incubated for eighteen days in a hatchery, its half-formed eyes, legs, feathers, and beak are all present and accounted for. More disgusting than its look, however, is the way it's eaten. First it is boiled. Then you crack open the shell and suck out the amniotic goodness. Then you dip the fetus into a little salt before tossing it down the hatch. And while it might not get you hot, just reading that should get you totally bothered. Of course, balut's aphrodisiacal properties are (supposedly) evidenced by the fact that a lot more of it is sold at night in the Philippines than during the day.

Give This Testicle a Resticle

Many kinds of testes are considered aphrodisiacs, but while most are merely foul, only one is potentially deadly. The fugu puffer fish is an expensive delicacy in Japan, even though—or maybe because—its organs contain lethal amounts of the poison tetrodotoxin. It's so difficult to prepare fugu safely that only specially licensed chefs can serve it. Unfortunately, that's of little comfort to the 20 or so Japanese diners who die every year from eating it anyway. Victims are fully paralyzed but remain conscious while they asphyxiate. (There are stories of fugu victims "waking up" after several days of deathlike paralysis—just before being cremated.)

✖ ✖ ✖

Found in the bark of an African tree, yohimbine is a popular "herbal" aphrodisiac known in pharmacology circles as a "selective competitive alpha2-adrenergic receptor antagonist." And while that doesn't make it a love potion per se, the rapid heart rate, high blood pressure, and overstimulation that result from high doses of the stuff do tend to *feel* like arousal. If those side effects aren't deterrent enough, however, consider that the drug is at its most effective when, um, directly injected in the you-know-where.

The Avocado "Down Low"

Somehow those Aztecs always seem to have their minds in the Mesoamerican gutter. So much so that they couldn't help but look at avocados (which admittedly hang in pairs) and conclude that they looked a lot like human testicles. In fact, they named the fruit-bearing tree the *ahuacatl*— or "testicle tree"—from which we get the English word *avocado*.

✖ ✖ ✖

The Snake King Completely restaurant in Guangdong, China, serves snake 100 ways, every one of which is supposedly a libido lifter. One popular favorite is a hot wine in which five snakes have been pickled. And while each snake should help on its own, they're supposedly even more effective with their numbers combined. After all, five is a lucky number in China, which should aid the drinker's chances of getting lucky. The Vietnamese also recognize the snake as an aphrodisiac, but prefer to swallow the still-throbbing heart of a cobra, with a little blood, from a shot glass. Luckily, they limit themselves to the lucky number one.

✖ ✖ ✖

Despite what its name might have you believe, the Spanish fly is neither Spanish, nor a fly. It's a beetle found primarily in southern Europe, which, when dried and crushed, makes a powder that's been used as an aphrodisiac since Roman times. It's actually an irritant, though, and when ingested and passed through the kidneys, the Spanish fly causes not arousal, but a painful swelling in the urinary tract. It has been said the Marquis de Sade fed bonbons laced with Spanish fly to women during an orgy, accidentally poisoning them. Who knew the marquis was so romantic? Now we can't speak for everyone, but hearing his tale definitely puts us in the mood for a good old-fashioned love story. . . .

09 Secret Romance Novelists

Before becoming the Vatican's top dog in 1458, Pius "the coolest-pope-in-history" II was an adventurer who traveled abroad on spy missions for the papacy, a smooth-talking diplomat, and a prolific writer. (Think of him as a kind of medieval James Bond with a slightly different collar.) His *Eurialus and Lucretia* is still read today, partly because it's an excellent early example of the epistolary novel, but mostly because it was written by a man who became pope—and it's *dirty*! Full of erotic imagery and surprisingly funny, it's comprised of salacious love letters between Lucretia (a married woman!) and Eurialus, servant to the Duke of Austria.

✖ ✖ ✖

One of America's greats, Joyce Carol Oates, has become synonymous with high-falutin' literature. So what's a writer oft-nominated for the Nobel Prize doing with pulpy romance novels like *Soul/Mate* and *The Stolen Heart* on her résumé? She never meant them to be: Written under pseudonyms "Rosamond Smith" (a feminization of Raymond Smith, her husband's name) and "Lauren Kelly," respectively, Oates was surprised and disappointed when her cover was blown by an anonymous source in 1987.

✹ ✹ ✹

If you're hoping for a heaving bosom or two, Benito Mussolini's *The Cardinal's Mistress,* serialized in a socialist newspaper long before he was an iron-fisted fascist leader, is bound to disappoint. While filled with purple prose, there's not a lot of action between the sheets. The story, about a cardinal's unhappy affair with a doomed woman, is mostly a soapbox for its author's anticlerical ranting. Sorry, Duce—propaganda makes terrible beach reading.

✹ ✹ ✹

In between all his Kurd-gassing, Kuwait-invading, and dissident-murdering, Iraq's own Great Dictator somehow found the energy to pen *Zabiba and the King.* Published anonymously after the first Gulf War, the book's authorship by Saddam was revealed by a Saudi newspaper in 2001. But was its provenance really a mystery? Not only was there zero criticism of the novel upon its release (the Iraqi press called it an "innovation in the history of novels"), the book's thinly veiled allegories were a total giveaway: A kindly leader (Saddam) loves a beautiful commoner (the Iraqi people) who is raped by her cruel husband (the United States).

✹ ✹ ✹

Just another breathy melodrama when it was published in 1981, *Sisters* sold poorly and was soon out of print. So why are paperback copies selling on the Internet today for $300?

Because *Sisters* makes its author, second lady of the United States and vocal gay marriage ban advocate Lynne Cheney, look like a big, fat hypocrite. It's a lesbian romance set in the Old West that features lots of romance and sex—both in and out of wedlock—and promotes contraceptive use for women who want to remain "free." Asked to comment on *Sisters* by the *New York Times*, Cheney said "I don't remember the plot." Apparently, gay marriage is even more controversial now than it was in 1981. And speaking of marriage . . .

10 Love and Marriage
(and the Baby Carriage)

While "jumping the broom" has become synonymous with the happy institution of marriage, the phrase is borrowed from a distinctly unhappy one: American slavery. Denied the right to marry legally, slaves improvised ceremonies with what they had on hand. Leaping over a broom handle came to symbolize a couple's leap of faith, a tradition still practiced in many African-American weddings today.

✹ ✹ ✹

Nothing like a little hard labor to get a marriage off on the right foot. The Italian custom of sawhorsing holds that neighbors must set up a log, sawhorse, and double-handled saw for newlyweds, who halve the log together. The thicker the log and duller the saw the better; the arduousness of sawhorsing symbolizes the equally mundane tasks a couple will have to endure together throughout their married life.

The Las Vegas of Victorian England

Long before Vegas was even a twinkle in a gangster's eye, Scotland was the quickie wedding capital of the world. It all started in 1753, when England passed Lord Hardwicke's Marriage Act, restricting kids under 21 from marrying without parental consent. Rough-and-tumble Scotland had no such rule, so lovers as young as 12 eloped across the border in droves. The first village they reached was Gretna Green, where thousands have since been married in a ram-shackle blacksmith's shop, their unions sealed by the now-traditional—and always ear-piercing—hammering of an anvil.

* * *

The Welsh, pushover romantics that they are, like to start weddings off with home invasions and kidnapping. (Hey, it's tradition!) Before the ceremony, the groom and groomsmen try to break into the bride's locked house. If they do—and the bride's own family hasn't kidnapped her first—she hides from the rowdy men, often in disguise as an old woman. Once apprehended, the bride is "kidnapped" and taken to the church—or if she's fast and wily, chased there.

* * *

Chances are, you've heard of polygamy, polyandry's better-known cousin: Mormons used to do it; Saudi Muslims can get away with it; relatively speaking, having a gaggle of wives is downright commonplace. But a woman having five husbands? In Tibet, where a father and his sons could share the same wife, it was the custom for centuries. Anthropologists suggest it was a matter of necessity. Because female infanticide was prevalent, there weren't a lot of women to go around, and because there isn't a lot of arable land in mountainous Tibet, polyandry kept the birth rate—and the starvation rate—low. When the

Chinese invaded in 1950, they put the kibosh on such nontraditional forms of marriage, not to mention a couple of other things.

Breaking Up Isn't So Hard to Do, After All

A 2001 study showed that 43 percent of first marriages in the U.S. end in divorce, and that number is only climbing. Soon, experts predict, more people will divorce each year than marry. Compare that to the U.S. divorce rate in 1940, which was just two divorcees per 1,000 people. In fact, untying the knot is so popular, we'll wager it's not long before it has its own set of wacky customs and traditions. Why does everything seem to *fall apart*? A good question, but an even better lead-in. . . .

4

Humpty Dumptys:
Victims of Precipitous Falls

While enormously popular in the 1920s and '30s, movie legend Charlie Chaplin's lefty politics and racy personal life (he had a habit of marrying teenagers) began to catch up with him during the increasingly conservative Cold War era. Accused of being a Communist, he found his visa revoked after a trip abroad in 1952 and vowed never to return, saying "I have no further use for America. I wouldn't go back there if Jesus Christ was president." In fact, he waited until Richard Nixon was president. Chaz made his triumphant return at the 1972 Academy Awards, where he was presented with a lifetime achievement Oscar.

✖ ✖ ✖

America's popular diet guru, Robert Atkins, and his

Grape Expectations

Ah, the vicissitudes of pop culture trendiness. America's favorite red wine in the '90s was famously name-checked by Cosmo Kramer on a 1997 *Seinfeld* episode: "I live for merlot." Riding high, merlot let fame go to its head—and its price tag. Overexposed and overpriced at an average $10/bottle, merlot's consumers started reaching for cheaper bottles imported from Argentina and Australia, and, when they realized those didn't taste so good, for Pinot Noirs and Cabernets. Sales dropped, reaching their nadir after 2004 Oscar winner *Sideways* kicked merlot while it was down. Humbled after its fall from grace, merlot is now a relative bargain—and as tasty as it ever was.

eponymous weight-loss program have suffered both figurative and literal falls from grace. Figurative: the diet's popularity waned once experts (like the American Heart Association) began pointing out that eating nothing but burgers-sans-bun can kill you. Not surprisingly, Atkins Nutritionals went belly-up in 2003. Literal: that same year, Atkins himself died from a fall on a slippery sidewalk. But if that hadn't gotten him, the low-carb king's cardiologist has since revealed, the 40 percent blockages in his coronary arteries eventually would've.

✖ ✖ ✖

When the English monarchy was restored to power in 1660, Cromwell crony and propagandist John Milton was arrested and fined heavily and lost his fortune. The only reason he escaped with his head was that he was going blind, which Charles II kindly looked upon as divine retribution. It was only then, poor, sightless, and obscure, that Milton wrote—or rather dictated—his blank verse epic *Paradise Lost*. (Talk about a fall from grace.) In 1667, he sold his masterwork to a flinty London bookseller for just ten pounds.

✖ ✖ ✖

Nowadays, Oscar Wilde is as remembered for his spectacular downfall as for his spectacular writing. Publicly harassed as a "sodomite" by the enraged father of a young lover, the famously flamboyant playwright sued the old man for libel. Rather than pay, he produced a few of Wilde's former bedfellows in court, and Wilde not only lost the case, but was charged with "gross indecency" for his troubles. The result was heartbreaking. Sentenced to two years' hard labor, he found himself waiting in a heavy rain, handcuffed, for transport to prison. "If this is the way Queen Victoria treats her prisoners," he quipped, "she doesn't deserve to have any." But it's not like Wilde was angry enough to start a hunger strike or anything. . . .

02 Just Water, Thanks:
The Greatest Hunger Strikers Ever

When it came to abstaining from things, Mohandas (Mahatma) Gandhi gave your average monk a run for his money: The Indian leader was a vegetarian, became celibate at age 36, and spent one day of each week in silence. But he was the Babe Ruth of hunger strikes. Not because of their length—his longest was 21 days—but due to their extreme, guilt-inducing effectiveness. In 1947, his fasting shamed the rioting city of Calcutta into peace, and in 1948 warring Muslims and Hindus in Delhi declared a truce to end his hunger strike.

✖ ✖ ✖

In his lifelong struggle against the giant grape growers of California, a favorite protest of labor rights hero Cesar Chavez was to stop eating. Ironic, perhaps, but he got results: Boycotts,

We Want Our Welsh TV

When it looked like Margaret Thatcher was about to renege on an election promise to create the first Welsh-language TV station, Gwynfor Evans did what any concerned member of Parliament would do: He threatened to go on a hunger strike. More surprising even than Evans's petulant tactic was that hard-nosed Thatcher gave in, and Sianel Pedwar Cymru (Channel Four Wales) began broadcasting in 1982. The station's biggest hit to date: SuperTed, the animated adventures of a magical teddy bear.

walkouts, and hunger strikes won his United Farm Workers of America a union contract and insurance benefits. But when dissenting UFW organizers went on a hunger strike of their own to protest Chavez having fired them, he got upset—and filed a $25 million libel suit against them.

✳ ✳ ✳

A divorced father and washed-up garbage collector at 40, Barry Horne was a midlife crisis waiting to happen. Forgoing the usual sports car purchase or affair with a younger woman, Horne instead launched a five-year campaign of firebombings against British companies he viewed as animal rights violators. In 1997 he was caught and received an 18-year jail sentence, the longest ever given to an animal rights protestor. Four hunger strikes followed in an attempt to force a public inquiry into animal lab testing—his longest was a record 68 days—to no avail. He died from starvation-induced kidney failure in 2001.

✳ ✳ ✳

What's so magical about magician David Blaine, anyway? His "tricks" consist mainly of absurd feats of endurance—encasing himself in ice for 66 hours, burying himself alive for a week—and while he name-checks Houdini as an influence, at least Houdini tried to escape. Blaine just tortures himself, not to mention his fans, in the process. A 2003 stunt suspended him 30 feet above a London park in a glass box, without food, for 44 days. (Sure, other folks have fasted for longer than that—but who else has done it for no reason?) Charitable Londoners decided if Blaine wanted to torture himself, they would do their best to help him: eggs, beer cans, and paint-filled balloons were all lobbed at the box, and one prankster used a radio-controlled helicopter to taunt Blaine with flying cheeseburgers. Call it a case of perfect celebrity justice.

03 Celebrity Justice:
Twenty "Trials of the Century"

Lately, media pundits and newsmakers have been dubbing things "trial of the century" like it's going out of style; according to ever-hyperbolic *USA TODAY*, Martha Stewart, Robert Blake, and Michael Jackson each had trials of the century—in 2005. Of course, we think that's just silly: So in the interest of setting the record straight, here are our top 20.

1906: Harry Thaw, the trust-funded son of a Pittsburgh industrialist, shoots Madison Square Garden architect Stanford White in the face—during a show at Madison Square Garden. Claiming White raped Thaw's wife, his lawyer wins an acquittal by arguing Thaw suffered from "dementia Americana," afflicting any American male whose wife's purity is violated.

1921: Anarchists Sacco and Vanzetti are sentenced to death on murder and robbery charges with scant evidence; intellectuals like George Bernard Shaw and Dorothy Parker argue the pair were guilty only of being radicals during an anti-Communist Red Scare. It doesn't matter; they hang.

1921: When a sickly trollop expires in Fatty Arbuckle's hotel room, the portly film star finds himself charged with rape and murder. Though acquitted, his career is ruined.

1924: Wealthy college boys Nathan Leopold and Richard Loeb murder a teenager just for fun, their "perfect crime" foiled when Leopold leaves his glasses with the body. Lawyer Clarence Darrow gives a 12-hour speech in their defense, sparing them from hanging.

1925: Darrow, the era's reigning liberal heavyweight, leaps to the defense of Tennessee schoolteacher John Scopes in the then- and now-legendary "Monkey Trial." Darrow loses the case despite much grandiose speechifying by him and prosecutor William Jennings Bryan; Scopes is fined a measly $100 for teaching evolution despite a state law banning it (though he never pays); and 80-plus years later we're still arguing about monkeys. Nice work, fellas.

1931: Nine black teenagers are falsely accused of gang-raping two white women in Alabama. The Scottsboro Boys—so known for where they were jailed—are first sentenced to death, then variously paroled or pardoned in two landmark Supreme Court decisions.

1935: The infant son of aviator Charles "Lucky" Lindbergh is kidnapped and murdered. Suspected killer Bruno Hauptmann's trial generates worldwide publicity. Convicted, Hauptmann is electrocuted in 1936.

1942: Swashbuckling film star Errol Flynn is tried and

acquitted of statutory rape, only furthering his rep as a devil-may-care ladies' man. (Or little girls' man, as it were.)

1945: The Nuremberg Trials. An international tribunal decides the fate of two dozen high-ranking Nazis. Journalists expecting monstrous defendants are surprised by the ordinariness of nasties like Hermann Göring, remarking on "the banality of evil."

1949: State department official Alger Hiss denies spying for Russia, despite seemingly damning evidence to the contrary. Because the statute of limitations on the spying charge itself has run out, he is tried and convicted of perjury.

1951: American Communists Julius and Ethel Rosenberg are convicted of passing U.S. nuclear secrets to Russia. Executed in 1953, the Rosenbergs' supposed guilt remains controversial.

1966: Hollywood glam-girl Hedy Lamarr shoplifts $86 worth of underwear from an L.A. department store. When confronted in the parking lot, she (reportedly) says, "The other stores let me do it!" After much ballyhoo on her behalf from an adoring public, she is acquitted.

1970: Charles Manson and his merry gang of murderers are convicted of murdering actress Sharon Tate and six others in highly publicized proceedings, further courting media attention by carving giant X's into their foreheads.

1976: Newspaper heiress Patty Hearst is convicted of robbing a federal bank as part of the radical Symbionese Liberation Army, the coverage of which sells a lot of newspapers. Coincidence? Or genius?

1982: John Hinckley Jr., the not-quite assassin of president Ronald Reagan, successfully pleads insanity, causing several states to rewrite laws regarding the insanity plea. Though he is now famous, Jodie Foster still cruelly refuses to date him.

1991: Hedy Lamarr, now 78 and living in Florida, is arrested for shoplifting again—this time for pocketing laxatives and eye drops. Rather than charging her, prosecutors ask her to please stop stealing things.

1992: "Iron" Mike Tyson is convicted of raping Miss Black Rhode Island, Desiree Washington. He converts to Islam in prison, exchanging "Iron" for a tamer sobriquet: Malik Abdul Aziz.

1992: A not guilty verdict for LAPD officers charged with beating black motorist Rodney King sparks devastating riots in Los Angeles that saw the deaths of 58 people.

1995: O. J. Simpson: "trial of the century" of the century? Let us break it down: The crime was sensational, but Harry Thaw's was more so. Cochran was compelling, but no Clarence Darrow. The trial's racial implications were troubling, but not like Scottsboro. Word.

1999: "Slick" William J. Clinton is (at least) the eighth U.S. president to engage in sexual misconduct while in office, the first to be forced to discuss it under oath, and his impeachment is the last of the 20th century's "trials of the century." His unfortunate fall, however, leads us to an altogether more pleasant kind of fall.

04 Having a "Great" Fall:
Facts and Figures About Terrifying Things That Happened in September, October, and November

On *November 20,* 1820, an 80-ton sperm whale rammed into and sank the *Essex,* a Nantucket whaling ship. Twenty years later, son of *Essex* survivor Owen Chase met a young Herman

Melville working aboard another whaling ship and regaled him with the tragic tale. On *October 19*, 1851, Melville published his own story about an aggressive sperm whale out for blood: *Moby-Dick*.

✳ ✳ ✳

Incidentally, there is at least one known instance of a whale destroying not a boat, but an automobile: On *November 12*, 1970, officials in Florence, Oregon, used dynamite to rid their beachfront of a 45-foot-long rotting whale carcass. Overzealous, they planted a half ton of it, and the resulting explosion sent whale chunks flying up to a quarter mile,

It's a Bird! It's a Plane! It's a . . . Bird Strike?

Bird strike, as the dangerous collision of airplanes and kamikaze birds is known, costs the aviation industry $600 million in damage annually and has resulted in 195 deaths since 1988. The deadliest single bird strike occurred on *October 4*, 1960, when a flock of starlings embedded themselves in all four engines of an Eastern Air Lines L-188 Electra, downing the plane into Boston Harbor and killing 62 people.

covering horrified news crews in blubber and caving in the roof of one poor fellow's car. Insert your own "Thar she blows!" joke here.

✳ ✳ ✳

A somewhat less disgusting but considerably more powerful explosion occurred on *November 1*, 1952, when the first hydrogen bomb was detonated. Code-named "Mike" (for megatons—10.4 of them), it was 450 times more powerful than the atomic bomb dropped on Nagasaki and erased the tiny Pacific atoll where it was tested. Irradiated coral rained on boats up to 30 miles away, resulting in several cases of radiation poisoning.

Another Avian Conspiracy

The Hooters restaurant chain was hatched on *October 4, 1983*, in Clearwater, Florida. Their heart-stopping chicken wings are hawked at more than 350 locations worldwide, a favorite of frat boys everywhere.

✳ ✳ ✳

One of the most notorious fraternity hazing deaths occurred at Kenyon College on *October 28*, 1905, when hooded Delta Kappa Epsilon brothers tied pledge Stuart Pierson to a railroad track and ran away, assuming no more trains were scheduled that evening. And we all know what happens when you assume.

✳ ✳ ✳

You never know what you're going to find, however, when you exhume; so paleontologists digging in Ethiopia were appropriately surprised on *November 24*, 1974, to uncover a 3.18 million-year-old female hominid of the genius Australopithecus—the oldest protohuman yet discovered. They name their famous skeleton "Lucy," a reference to the Beatles song "Lucy in the Sky with Diamonds." ("I'm Looking Through You" seems a more appropriate Beatles nod, but whatever.) "Diamonds" it is. . . .

05 Ice, Ice, Baby—Diamonds

The world's largest cut diamond is the pear-cut, 530-carat Cullinan I, which also goes by a more elegant name: "Great Star of Africa." Africa's Great Star, it rather goes without saying, resides in Europe. It's part of Britain's Crown Jewels.

✖ ✖ ✖

Way back when, diamonds didn't need advertising campaigns. The Greeks, poets that they were, believed them to be splinters of fallen stars or the teardrops of gods. Plato himself guessed they were living beings that embodied celestial spirits. And with publicity like that, who needed a shill? By 1932, however, diamonds had lost some of their luster, with annual worldwide sales at a measly $100,000. Diamond giant De Beers decided what their product needed was a new legend, and with the help of Madison Avenue, that's just what they created. Named "slogan of the 20th century" by *Advertising Age* magazine, the "a diamond is forever" campaign convinced millions of wooing suitors that there was only one way to express their undying devotion—and it wasn't with a sapphire or a ruby. The diamond engagement ring became a marketing blockbuster, transforming diamonds into a $2 billion-a-year business by 1979.

It Really Is Made from People

Diamonds are forever, the saying goes—and now you can be a diamond forever, too. For just a few thousand bucks, Chicago's LifeGem company will turn the cremated remains of your favorite pet or loved one into a reasonably high-quality "memorial diamond" suitable for mounting in a ring or necklace. The process replicates the awesome heat and pressure needed to create a natural diamond, but instead of millions of years, it takes about six months. One caveat: The diamonds tend to be a rather unappetizing yellow.

✖ ✖ ✖

When Elizabeth Taylor sat down to write her memoir in 2001, she didn't waste any pages on her acting career or eight marriages. She wrote about her diamonds. *My Love Affair with Jewelry* is an autobiography refracted through the facets of her world-renowned collection, from the diamond tiara given to her by film producer Mike Todd (hubby #3) to the jaw-dropping, pear-shaped Krupp diamond gifted by Richard Burton (hubby #6 and #7). The Krupp diamond, by the way, was at the time the 56th largest in the world and one of the most precious stones in private hands. Some girls have all the luck.

✳ ✳ ✳

We've all seen the less-than-subtle product placements in movies—but in novels? In 2001, literary types were shocked to discover that author Fay Weldon's latest novel, *The Bulgari Connection*, had more than just a titular connection to the jewelry manufacturer. Bulgari had, in fact, paid Weldon to write it. That explains the dozens of near-sexual descriptions of their products found within ("it was a sleek modern piece . . . the mount following the irregular contours of the thin worn bronze"), but not why a respectable, Booker Prize–nominated writer would accept such a payoff. In her defense, a defiant Weldon said, "I don't care. They never give me the Booker prize anyway!" Having earned so much critical condemnation, she's unlikely to get one now. Unless she chooses a pseudonym. . . .

16 Great Pseudonyms

In Proverbs it's written that "a good name is rather to be chosen than great riches." Shakespeare agreed, writing in *Othello* that "good name in man and woman . . . is the immediate jewel of their souls." Which is why, for all you Nedberts and Poindexters out there, sometimes it's best to just cut bait and start over. Here are our all-time favorite pseudonyms—from art, music, and science—because like the Book of Ecclesiastes says: "A good name is better than precious ointment." (Or something.)

✻ ✻ ✻

Not familiar with the *Dionaea muscipula*? You might know it better by its wicked nickname: the Venus flytrap. While that's a plenty-cool pseudonym these days, the misogynistic botanists who came up with it in the 17th century didn't mean

V. I. Diddy

Revolutionary Bolshevik leader Vladimir Ilyich Ulyanov had over 160 aliases during his life—of which "Lenin" was only the last—nearly rivaling the pseudonymousness of revolutionary rap mogul Sean P. Combs. Combs (a.k.a. "Puff Daddy," "Puffy," etc.) explained a recent switch from "P. Diddy" to plain ole "Diddy" by saying "I felt the 'P' was getting between me and my fans."

it to be flattering; they tried to draw a connection between the

Losing My Religion

Is it just us, or do celebrities think that Jewish-sounding names are simply not hard rocking enough for the limelight? If that's the case, it would explain how mild-mannered schoolteacher Chaim Witz became rock group KISS's frontman and "devil horns" gesture inventor Gene Simmons; how Londoner Saul Hudson became ax master Slash; and how Ralph Lipschitz, Bronx-born son of Jewish immigrants, became the fashion designer of choice for old-money country clubbers: Ralph Lauren. As for one Herschel Pinkus Yerucham Krustofski, however, we'll let the philosophers decide how he found his true calling—as Krusty the Clown.

Alan Smithee

We've all done things we're not proud of, but usually we have to 'fess up and take the blame. Not so in Hollywood, where directors have been using the pseudonym "Alan Smithee"—an anagram of "the alias men"—to hide from their mistakes since 1968. At least 40 films, music videos, and adapted-for-TV movies have been credited to the infamous Mr. Smithee, making him one of the most prolific helmers in the movie biz. Highlights from his résumé include gems like *Bloodsucking Pharaohs in Pittsburgh,* Whitney Houston's "I Will Always Love You" music video, and the Scott Baio heartwarmer *I Love N.Y.* Like him or not, you've got to admit: Smithee's got range.

flytrap's method of luring and devouring insects and what they saw as the world's other great temptress: the vagina.

✖ ✖ ✖

Controversy lingers over the true name of Arthur C. Clarke's fictional HAL 9000, the always unflappable, sometimes deadly computer from his 2001 trilogy. Clarke insists it stands for "Heuristically programmed ALgorithmic computer," but sci-fi nerds (sorry . . . *buffs*) claim that "HAL" is a not-so-subtle code for "IBM" (H-I, A-B, L-M). If computers (now ubiquitous), ciphers (*The Da Vinci Code*), and sci-fi (*Matrix,* anyone?) are no longer the sole province of nerd-dom, one thing is and shall always remain so. . . .

07 Periodically Speaking:
Highlights from the Periodic Table

ALUMINUM (AL)

According to legend, the goldsmith who first refined bauxite into aluminum hammered a dinner plate out of the stuff and presented it to the Roman emperor Tiberius. Concerned that proliferation of this shiny new metal would render his vast storehouse of gold and silver worthless, Tiberius had the goldsmith beheaded.

SULFUR (S)

Called "brimstone" throughout English translations of the Bible, sulfur may be the only element that keeps penitent Christians up at night: In Genesis it rains down on the naughty denizens of Sodom and Gomorrah, killing them; and Revelations describes hell as being both hot (from all the fire) as well as stinky (from all the sulfur). But sulfur keeps secular folk up at night, too— its release into the atmosphere by petrochemical plants is a leading cause of acid rain.

Murder Was the Case:
ARSENIC (AS) THROUGH HISTORY

Arsenic has many uses, the most popular of which, historically, have been suicide, fratricide, matricide, regicide—and just plain old murder. Also known as "the king of poisons" (or "the poison of kings"), it kills quickly, discreetly, and untraceably, making it the most popular choice for upper-crust grudge holders and inheritance seekers since the Greeks discovered hemlock. (One famous victim is Napoléon, thought to have been fed arsenic by one of his entourage.) It's no longer possible to play off such deaths as accidental, though. In 1836, chemist James Marsh perfected an effective test for arsenic poisoning.

IRIDIUM (IR)

This element was the clue that cracked one of history's biggest murder cases: What killed the dinosaurs? Turns out the layer of sediment laid down 65 million years ago—right on top of all the dino skeletons we excavate today—is full of iridium, rare on the surface of the Earth but intriguingly common in asteroids. This effectively put to rest a host of other extinction theories, ranging from a nearby supernova dissolving the atmosphere to a decrease in brain size, which, yielding very special dinosaurs, made them more susceptible to predators.

TANTALUM (TA)

Its name was inspired by the mythical Greek Tantalus, who was condemned to stand for all eternity with perfect fruit growing just out of reach. Tantalum is similarly nonreactive and is used widely in making surgical equipment because of its immunity to corrosion by bodily fluids.

RADIUM (RA)

This element's soft blue luminescence earned it a name derived from the Latin word *radius* for "ray," as in ray of light. For a while radium was used to paint glow-in-the-dark instrument panels and clock faces until the painters noticed that it seemed to kill them. In fact, despite prior warnings from radium discoverer Marie Curie about not putting radioactive things in your mouth, the painters continued to shape their tiny brushes with their lips. Told you so!

POLONIUM (PO)

So, how many Polacks did it take to discover polonium? Just one: native daughter Marie Curie. The famous scientist named it in 1898 for her then-beleaguered homeland, which was tangled in a web of fighting among Austria, Russia, and Germany. Speaking of tangled webs . . .

⌐⌐ Web-Based Trivia:
Choice Pit Stops on the Information Superhighway

When Ray Tomlinson invented the software that allowed computers to send messages to one another in 1971—back when the Internet linked computers at just 15 sites—he could hardly have realized how significant this new technology would be. But unlike other legendary first communications ("Mr. Watson, come here; I want you" were Alexander Graham Bell's first words over a telephone), Tomlinson says his historic first e-mail was "completely forgettable." (He has, in fact, forgotten it.) His best guess: "Qwertyuiop."

✷ ✷ ✷

Since the first Web browser was disseminated in 1990, the number of registered Web sites on the Internet has grown exponentially—from just 16,000 in 1992 to more than 50 million in 2005. That, of course, explains why it's become harder to find an available domain name that makes any sense at all. Despite the many trillions of possible names for a Web site (that's including all combinations of numbers and letters up to 22 characters in length), there are only so many English words. As of 2000, only about 1,700 one-word English domain names were still available. It's just this kind of unfriendly math that's given rise to "cybersquatting," which is how Houston businessman Marc Ostrofsky bought the domain "business.com" for $150,000 in 1996 and sold it for

The Search for Intelligent Life on the Internet

Sure, computers are big time savers; but they're even bigger time wasters. Fact is, however obsessively you check your e-mail, gamble on the Internet, or play video games, your CPU processor spends more time each day doing nothing than doing something. In 1999, one group came up with a way to put all that wasted processor time to use: by looking for aliens. Each day SETI@Home receives a huge chunk of data from a Puerto Rican radio telescope aimed into space, breaks it down into much smaller chunks (about 250 kilobytes apiece) and distributes those to more than five million Internet-connected participants worldwide. During what would otherwise be down time, these millions of processors analyze their data chunks for irregularities that—just maybe—could be radio transmissions from aliens. As of 2005, the project had logged a comprehension-defying two million days of

$7.5 million just four years later. He got a sweet deal for "eFlowers.com," too: $25,000 plus monthly flower deliveries to his wife—for life. (See also p. 121.)

✳ ✳ ✳

Contrary to popular legend, Al Gore did not invent the Internet. Instead, credit the Brit Tim Berners-Lee with the creation, in 1980, of a hyperlinked filing system that formed the basis of what he christened the "World Wide Web." There would've been far less confusion as to the Web's inventor, however, if Berners-Lee had just stuck with his original name for it: "TIM"—an acronym for "The Information Mine."

✳ ✳ ✳

In 1998, then-upstart Google.com founders Sergey Brin and Larry Page approached Yahoo with a humble merger offer but were brusquely sent packing. Five years later, Google was worth an estimated $20 billion. Yahoo has to live with the fact that their main rival could once have been acquired with a handful of stock—just as many of us have to live with embarrassing tattoos acquired while intoxicated. . . .

aggregate computing time, earning SETI@Home a place in the *Guinness Book of World Records* as the largest computation in history. (Extraterrestrials found: zero.)

09 Tattoo Timeline

3300 BCE: Ötzi the Iceman dies in the Austrian Alps, where his frozen body is discovered by hikers in 1991 CE, making him the world's oldest mummy. His 57 tattoos—straight lines and small crosses, mostly—are believed to be therapeutic, possibly used to treat osteoarthritis. Hey, if you were 5,291 years old, you'd be a little stiff, too.

2800 BCE: The ancient Egyptians: Is there anything they can't do? In addition to inventing writing, surgery, and beekeeping, they also popularize tattooing as an art form, which spreads from Greece to China. (Oh, yeah—they invented the flushable toilet, too.)

921 CE: Islamic scholar Ibn Fadlan meets Vikings on a journey from Baghdad to Scandinavia and describes them as vulgar, dirty, and covered from neck to toe with tattoos. Awww . . . isn't that Swede?

1600: Unlawful intercourse by Indian priests is punished by tattooing. Doesn't sound so bad? Try having a big vagina branded on your forehead for life. (Makes you wonder what Hester was complaining about in *The Scarlet Letter*.)

1700: Obeying the letter of the law—if not the spirit—middle-class Japanese adorn themselves in full-body tattoos when a law is passed that only royals can wear ornate clothing.

1770: Captain Cook returns from a voyage to the South Pacific with a unique souvenir: a tattooed Polynesian named Omai. He's an overnight sensation in fad-crazy London and starts a tattooing trend among upper-class poseurs. Between passionate declarations that he is "not an animal" Omai also manages to introduce the word *tattoo* into our Western lexicon, from the Tahitian *tatau,* "to mark."

1802: By now, tattooing has caught on with sailors throughout the Royal Navy, and there are tattoo artists in almost every British port. Especially popular are Crucifixion scenes, tattooed on the upper back to discourage flogging by pious superiors.

1891: American Samuel O'Reilly "borrows" Edison's electric pen design to patent a nearly identical machine that tattoos. (Way to stand on the shoulders of giants, Sam.) Its basic design—moving coils, a tube, and a needle bar—is still used to today, so remember, kids: That's 19th-century technology they're repeatedly stabbing you with.

1919: The troublemaker protagonist of Franz Kafka's short story "In the Penal Colony" finally gets the law drilled into him—literally—by its fatal, 12-hour inscription into his skin.

1955: Robert Mitchum makes the tattoo cool again in the movie *Night of the Hunter,* playing a sociopathic traveling preacher with "love" and "hate" inked on his knuckles. Popular modern variants include "rock/roll" and "love/math."

1961: Hepatitis B makes the tattoo not cool again, an outbreak of which is linked to tattoo parlors in New York City. Parlors are outlawed in the Big Apple until 1997.

2005: Pop culture helps tattoos become more popular in the West than at any time in recorded history, with more than 39 million North Americans sporting one. It all comes back to Austrian Ötzi and his 57 tattoos. It might've taken almost

6,000 years, but tattooing and the West are in love again. And speaking of history's great reunions . . .

10 Getting Put Back Together Again:
Great Reunions

Perhaps no reunion of the 20th century had been more hotly anticipated than that of East and West Germany in 1990; overjoyed Berliners tearing down the wall that separated them has become the icon for the end of the Cold War. And at first everything was roses. Families caught on both sides of the Iron Curtain were reunited, and the East German state held the first and only free elections in its history, the major mandate of which was to dissolve the East German state. But nearly 20 years later, the honeymoon is over; former East and West are bickering about what most married couples bicker about: money. High unemployment, the failure of Soviet-era industries, and unchecked migration out of East Germany is costing West Germany upwards of €100 billion in aid annually.

Republics Behaving Badly: THE PARENT TRAP

Not coincidentally, it was a German, Erich Kästner, who wrote *The Parent Trap* (*Das Doppelte Lottchen,* adapted for American film and television at least five times). Identical twins (the German people) have been separated since birth by their divorced parents (the Federal Republic of Germany and the German Democratic Republic). Determined to bring them together again, the twins must chase away a rival for their father's affection (the Soviet Bloc) by convincing her that living with the naughty twins isn't worth it (via mass demonstrations and civil unrest).

Art Who?

If anyone has broken up and gotten back together more times than Taylor and Burton, it's Simon & Garfunkel. The first time was in 1964, before they even had a career to speak of. Their first album, *Wednesday Morning, 3 AM*, had flopped bigtime, and they only decided to reunite when their single "The Sound of Silence" unexpectedly became a massive hit. When Art Garfunkel started to pursue acting in favor of his musical collaborations with Paul Simon, they broke up again, in 1969. Since then, the cantankerous couple have reunited (if only briefly) four times, most famously at a 1981 concert in Central Park, attended by 500,000 rabid fans.

✷ ✷ ✷

Germans can enjoy a bit of schadenfreude in that their reunion, despite its troubles, has already lasted far longer than that of Elizabeth Taylor and Richard Burton, who remarried in 1975 after having divorced one another just 16 months prior. They were back on the marital bliss wagon for less than a year, redivorcing in 1976 after Burton fell off the not-drinking-alcohol wagon.

✷ ✷ ✷

Forget today's modern Civil War reenactments; they're as meaningful as a Disneyland Ice Capades show compared to the first reenactment, one of history's greatest reunions. In 1913, fifty years after the momentous Battle of Gettysburg, 50,000 Confederate and Union veterans returned to camp together on the fields where they had once been locked in mortal combat. The highlight was a reenactment of the infamous Pickett's Charge, in which more than 3,000 men died in a matter of minutes. But this time, instead of meeting one another with bayonets and artillery fire, the old men threw down their weapons and embraced one another. Now that's a story that warms our hearts. And speaking of hearts . . .

5

01 *Your Cheatin' Heart*

LITERATI

Charles Dickens's wife, Catherine, ended up having a nervous breakdown that was probably attributable to postpartum depression. But it may also have been related to her husband's inveterate infidelity, including a possible love affair with Catherine's sister Mary (who inspired Little Nell in *The Old Curiosity Shop*).

✖ ✖ ✖

Dorothy Parker cheated repeatedly on both of her husbands, and she never really made a point of hiding it. Forgive us, but if everyone Dorothy Parker knew were laid end to end, we wouldn't be at all surprised.

✖ ✖ ✖

William Faulkner's childhood sweetheart, Estelle, divorced her first husband in

Happily Ever After

Happy marriages are rare in the world of letters, but few marriages were more blessed than that of Mark Twain and his wife, Olivia Langdon. The two married in 1870, just after Twain's *The Innocents Abroad* made him famous. And until Livy's death 34 years later, the Twains remained consistently, faithfully in love.

order to marry Faulkner, but he proved to be a poor choice.

Besides having an affair with the memorably named Meta Carpenter, Faulkner often complained that his wife just didn't *get* all the toil and sweat and misery of the authorial life. No doubt! All that sitting and writing stuff down is hard work.

NON-AMERICAN POLITICIANS

After Joseph Stalin's first wife, Ekaterina, died in 1907, Stalin said he would never feel love for another person (perhaps to prove it, he later had her family shot). But for being the only creature he ever loved, he treated Ekaterina pretty poorly—she had to suffer his notorious temper tantrums as well as his chronic infidelity.

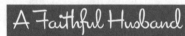

A Faithful Husband

When Winston Churchill married Clementine Hozier in 1908, a family friend said, "Their marriage will fail because Winston is not the marrying kind." False prophesy. Churchill never had another love—well, unless you count gin. Clementine, dignified and shy and comparably sober, was no retiring violet, either: During the Blitz, she often joined Winston on tours of bombed-out London.

ROYALTY

Jahangir, the fourth Mogul emperor of India, supposedly had 300 wives (296 more than allowed by the Islamic religion he espoused). And yet, he couldn't stay faithful to them: He also had 5,000 female concubines and 1,000 male ones.

✻ ✻ ✻

The French elevated the position of royal mistress to very near that of queen. Louis XV, for instance, mourned the death of his second mistress for months before Jeanne-Antoinette Poisson came along. Despite 1) being married, and 2) having a last name that literally translates to "fish," Jeanne-Antoinette appealed to Louis. He brought her to live at the palace and for the next 19 years, Madame de Pompadour, as she was known, reigned over Louis XV's court. She wielded so much power, in fact, that an adviser once said, "The mistress is prime minister."

✶ ✶ ✶

Catherine the Great, Russia's empress from 1762 to 1796, *did* have a lot of lovers—but given that her marriage to emotionally stunted, impotent, and inbred-to-the-point-of-insanity Peter III was never consummated, who can blame her? And sure, Catherine kept a secret room filled with erotic paintings and engravings. But for the last time: She did *not* die in a botched attempt to make love to a horse.

✶ ✶ ✶

Talk about moving up in the world: Nell Gwynn, English king Charles II's best-known (but by no means only!) mistress, was born in a London alley to a woman who ran a

Happily Ever After (Sort of)

Franz Ferdinand, who was once heir to the Austro-Hungarian Empire, had very little to recommend him as a person. Spoiled and ill-mannered, Franz was so disliked by the Viennese elite he was known as "the loneliest man in Vienna." But unlike most every royal in Europe, he loved his wife, Sophie, a middle-class woman his family thought beneath him. But marrying Sophie was the best decision he ever made. The worst decision he ever made, of course, was taking Sophie to Sarajevo on June 28, 1914, the couple's 14th wedding anniversary, where they were both assassinated by anarchist Gavrilo Princip. Franz Ferdinand's last words were an attempt to comfort his wife: "It is nothing," he assured her. But it was something indeed: Their murders sparked World War I.

brothel. Before settling down in extramarital bliss with Charles, Gwynn was one of Europe's first professional actresses.

PRESIDENTS

Franklin Delano Roosevelt's last words were "I have a terrific headache." (Indeed, he'd just had a cerebral hemorrhage.) However, he spoke them not to his wife, Eleanor, but to his mistress, Lucy. And while Roosevelt is known to have had a number of affairs, it's the (unproven) speculation about Eleanor's infidelity that tends to grab the headlines.

✻ ✻ ✻

Presidents known or believed to have had illegitimate children include Thomas Jefferson, Grover Cleveland, and Warren G. Harding.

✻ ✻ ✻

Speaking of Harding: After Carrie Phillips, with whom Harding had carried on a 15-year relationship, threatened to release their love letters to the newspapers, Harding's campaign paid her $20,000 to keep quiet. And you thought Nixon was dirty. . . .

✻ ✻ ✻

Of course, Nixon *was* dirty. Although it isn't exactly pleasant to picture, it's fairly well established that Nixon repeatedly cheated on his wife, Pat.

✻ ✻ ✻

DNA tests have now confirmed that Thomas Jefferson fathered children with his slave, Sally Hemings. Rumors have long swirled, though, that George Washington fathered a child with a slave, too. According to the story, Washington had a brief relationship in 1784 with a slave named Venus, who was owned by Washington's brother. Nine months later, Venus had a son named West Ford, who became a prominent freedman in northern Virginia.

SCIENTISTS

Albert Einstein is a hero and a genius and everything, but he wasn't the World's Greatest Husband. "I treat my wife," he once wrote in a love letter to his mistress, Elsa (who was also his first cousin), "as an employee whom I cannot fire." Eventually, though, he *did* fire her, divorcing her and then marrying Elsa—with whom he lived happily, if not entirely faithfully, ever after.

✖ ✖ ✖

Sigmund Freud never named the particular complex from which he apparently suffered. The Oedipus complex has to do with boys and their moms; the Electra complex involves fathers and daughters; but what's the one where you cheat on your wife, Martha, with her sister, Minna? Speaking of Freud . . .

02 And You Thought Freud Was Nuts:
Notes from the Early Days of Psychology

Hydrotherapy, or the use of water to cure sickness, has been around for a long time—Hippocrates (of Oath fame) prescribed bathing in clean spring water to cure all manners of disease. But it didn't gain favor as a treatment for mental illness until the 19th century. Mental hospitals began using hot mineral-water baths to relax anxious patients and cold baths to invigorate depressed ones. But we're not talking about an evening alone with champagne and Mr. Bubble. The "water cure," as it was known, often involved hours-long baths at frigid or near-scalding temperatures. Still, it was better than getting, say, malaria.

✖ ✖ ✖

Before the advent of antibiotics, syphilis was basically untreatable, and late-stage syphilitics often suffered from a neurological condition somewhere between bipolar disease and schizophrenia. So how to cure it? Why, with malaria, of course. Beginning in 1917, Austrian neurologist Julius von Jauregg injected his syphilitic patients with malaria (how he got the idea to do this we can only imagine). After a series of terrible fevers (which seemed to eradicate the syphilis), the treatment managed to calm patients down. Malarial therapy spread like—well, like malaria—and in 1927, von Jauregg received a Nobel Prize. *For intentionally giving crazy people malaria.* Remarkably, malarial fever therapy remained in use until the late 1960s.

Some scholars have argued that everyone from Abraham Lincoln (unlikely) to Ivan the Terrible (very possible) to Al Capone (definitely died of it) suffered from syphilis.

✖ ✖ ✖

In 1927, Polish psychologist Manfred Sakel observed that people in insulin comas tended to be a lot less agitated than schizophrenics. Why, he wondered, don't we inject massive doses of insulin into schizophrenic people? And so he did.

Indeed, insulin shock therapy calmed the schizophrenics down considerably—and only killed them about 1 percent of the time—but its long-term efficacy was questionable. Sakel's therapy is still used in parts of Eastern Europe, but it was replaced in the United States by the now rarely used (yet equally questionable) electric shock therapy.

Trepanation

It's a surgery you quite literally need like a hole in your head. Trepanation (which sounds like *trepidation* for a reason) is a form of surgery that drills a hole in the skull without (hopefully!) piercing the brain's membrane. Evidence of trepanation has been found everywhere from ancient Greece to pre-European South America.

Modern psychosurgery got its start with it in 1935, when Egas Moniz invented the prefrontal lobotomy. Although the surgery had a death rate of 6 percent and a brain damage rate of 100 percent, Moniz somehow managed to win the Nobel Prize in Medicine for it in 1949. Perhaps he gave prefrontal lobotomies to members of the nominating committee.

But Moniz was a veritable Dr. Salk compared to Walter Freeman, an American whose no-frills lobotomy led to the lobotomization of almost 50,000 people (including John F. Kennedy's sister Rosemary). Freeman's lobotomy involved exactly two tools: an ice pick and a mallet. He would pound the ice pick into the skull above the tear duct and wiggle it around until the brain damage was done. Frankly, it's enough to give us tomophobia (i.e., a morbid fear of surgical operations). And speaking of long words ending in *phobia* . . .

03 Phobias!

(Three Pages of Nothing to Fear but Fears Themselves!)

TRISKAIDEKAPHOBIA

What You Fear: the number 13

Real Reason to Fear It: Well, the whole world can't be wrong. From Turkey to Paris, 13 has been reviled for centuries.

Related Phobias: Arithmophobia (the fear of numbers more generally—and a rational phobia if ever there was one)

Noted Sufferer: Composer Arnold Schoenberg intentionally misspelled Aaron in his opera *Moses und Aron* to keep the title from having 13 letters; morbidly afraid of 13, he died on Friday the 13th.

Surprising Fact: Schoenberg might not have been nuts. A 1993 British study showed that Friday the 13th really *is* bad for your health—according to the study, hospital admissions rise as much as 52 percent.

ARACHIBUTYROPHOBIA

What You Fear: peanut butter sticking to the roof of your mouth

Real Reason to Fear It: About .5 percent of the American population is allergic to peanuts, and for reasons researchers don't really understand, the number is growing.

Related Phobias: Pnigophobia (fear of choking or being smothered)

Noted Sufferers: none—it's hard to imagine anyone with such a fear rising to prominence.

Surprising Fact: The fact that such a phobia has a scientific name strikes us as fairly surprising.

PHILEMAPHOBIA

What You Fear: kissing

Real Reason to Fear It: One might mix up "kissing" with "Kissinger," who is scary indeed.

Related Phobias: Myxophobia (fear of slime)

Noted Sufferers: Well, after the hullabaloo with Judas, one couldn't blame Jesus for being a little kiss-phobic.

Surprising Fact: Kissing *is* occasionally fatal. Eighth-century Chinese poet Li Po supposedly drowned after leaning out of a boat in an attempt to kiss the moon's reflection. (He had, it rather goes without saying, been drinking.)

HYDROPHOBIA

What You Fear: water—or, worse still, bathing in it

Real Reason to Fear It: There are plenty: giardia, E. coli, drowning.

Related Phobia: Urophobia (fear of passed water, i.e., pee)

Noted Sufferer: Prussian emperor Frederick the Great, known to his intimates as Frederick-the-incredibly-foul-smelling-because-he-refuses-to-ever-bathe-in-his-entire-life-but-still-kinda-Great. Frederick also made his coffee with champagne instead of water.

Surprising Fact: Hydrophobia is also a symptom for late-stage rabies infection—unable to swallow, victims panic when presented with liquid. And that, Scout, is why Atticus had to shoot the dog.

URANOPHOBIA

What You Fear: heaven, or going to heaven

Real Reason to Fear It: You hate harps, or worry that having wings will only worsen your fear of flying (aviophobia).

Related Phobias: Zeusophobia (fear of God. Or gods. Or Zeus).

Noted Sufferers: Voltaire, maybe. On his deathbed, the Enlightenment philosopher was asked to repudiate the devil. Voltaire responded, "Is this a time to be making enemies?"

Surprising Fact: that anyone would be afraid of heaven. In fact, the vast majority of folks would qualify as uranophilics, or heaven lovers. And speaking of philias . . .

04 Philias!
The Great Loves of Great Lives

CROSSED EYES

René "I think, therefore I am" Descartes had a fetish for women with crossed eyes (now known as *strabismus*), which—as it turns out—served as a proof for his belief in free will. As a young boy, Descartes had a cross-eyed playmate with whom he was infatuated, which he took to be the cause of his fondness for cross-eyed women later in life. When he remembered his young strabismal love, Descartes was able to rid himself of the fetish—thus proving that humans need not be a slaves to their eccentric passions. Good for Descartes, sure, but too bad for cross-eyed girls. In a time when strabismus was often seen as a curse, they could have used more guys like René.

Others Fond of Crossed Eyes: Mary Todd Lincoln, perhaps—since her husband, Abraham, suffered from strabismus.

DOGS

Think your pals who send you Christmas letters ostensibly written by their German shepherds are obsessed with their pups? Well, just thank the heavens you weren't tight with Tokugawa Tsunayoshi, the shogun of Japan from 1680 to 1709. Tsunayoshi really, *really* dug dogs. Born in the year of the dog, Tsunayoshi owned some 50,000 of them, and they were all fed gourmet meals of dried fish and rice. He also made harming a dog (not killing—*harming*) a crime punishable by death.

Others Fond of Dogs: It's a far cry from Tsunayoshi, but Ozzy and Sharon Osbourne own a brood of nearly a dozen dogs.

PIGEONS

Nikola Tesla, the Serbian inventor who made countless contributions to the science of electricity, had a hard life. Every time he invented or improved something (alternating current (AC), for instance), his ideas were generally stolen. Also, he suffered from periodic nervous breakdowns and never had very close relationships—with people, that is. But pigeons were a different story. Late in his life, Tesla grew inordinately fond of pigeons. He fed them by the thousands and even fell in love with one particular white pigeon. Of her, Tesla wrote, "I loved that pigeon. I loved her as a man loves a woman, and she loved me."

Others Fond of Pigeons: Mike Tyson (who has said they are

his only friends), Pablo Picasso (who named a daughter Paloma, Spanish for pigeon), and Charles Darwin (who was an active member of a London pigeon club). Speaking of whom . . .

BARNACLES

The same obsessive powers of observation that led to Charles Darwin's great discoveries were for many years focused on, um, barnacles. After his historic voyage on the *Beagle* but before he wrote the evolution-introducing *On the Origin of Species,* Darwin became fixated on barnacles and other marine invertebrates. Over the course of eight years, he obsessively studied, drew, and dissected barnacles, eventually publishing four (*four!*) books on the creatures. He finally abandoned barnacles in the mid-1850s and gathered his thoughts on evolution, publishing in 1859 *On the Origin of Species,* which finally won him the fame his barnacle books had not. Which just goes to show that where there's a neurotic, intractable will, there's a way. And . . .

05 Where There's a Way, There's a Will:
Unusual Wills

When Irish playwright and Nobel laureate George Bernard Shaw died in 1950, he left a substantial share of his estate to creating a new English alphabet. Shaw felt the Latin alphabet was "hopelessly inadequate," and wanted to replace it with one that contained between 40 and 50 characters.

✖ ✖ ✖

William Shakespeare famously bequeathed his wife his "second-best bed," which seems pretty cruel. But in all likelihood, the second-best bed was the one they shared—and therefore a final romantic gesture.

✖ ✖ ✖

The comedian Jack Benny did even better by his wife. The day after Benny's death, his wife, Mary, received one long-stemmed rose from a florist.

You're Like Sunshine on a Cloudy Day

German poet Heinrich Heine was not so kind to his wife. His last will and testament bequeathed his entire estate to his wife, Eugenie—as long as she remarried. Why force her to remarry? So that "there will be at least one man to regret my death."

The next day, another came. When Mary called to ask about the deliveries, she learned that Benny had stipulated in his will "one perfect red rose daily for the rest of Mary's life."

✖ ✖ ✖

The only heir to the Singer sewing machine fortune, Daisy Singer Alexander was an eccentric woman who enjoyed dropping bottles with messages inside into the River Thames. In June of 1937, Alexander wrote a note reading, "To avoid all confusion, I leave my entire estate to the lucky person who finds this bottle," sealed it in a bottle, and threw it into the river. Singer died in 1940. In 1949, a San Francisco dishwasher named Jack Wrum was walking along the beach and happened across a sealed bottle. As a result of the note inside, he inherited $8 million.

✖ ✖ ✖

John Keats died when he was just 25—had he survived, he might have become the greatest writer of his era. As it was, he

How to Win Friends and Influence People (Postmortem)

If you've always wanted to be remembered but your chances of achieving fame in life look bleak, take a lesson from Canadian Charles Vance Millar. Although a very successful lawyer, Millar didn't achieve notoriety until 1926, when he died. He bequeathed much of his estate to whichever woman in Canada had the most children in the 10 years following his death. The will survived several attempts to annul it, and four Toronto women—each of whom had nine babies during what came to be called the "Great Stork Derby"—eventually inherited shares of his $750,000 estate.

left behind a few brilliant, celebrated poems, most famously "Ode on a Grecian Urn." Keats's last will and testament also seems to have been his last, and shortest, poem. His will was a single line of perfect iambic pentameter: "My chest of books divide amongst my friends."

✳ ✳ ✳

Del Close, who founded Chicago's ImprovOlympic theater and taught dozens of *Saturday Night Live* cast members, died of cancer in 1999. He willed his skull to Chicago's Goodman Theatre, in hopes that after his death he might be able to play Yorick in *Hamlet*. Awfully brilliant—but we can't help but think that he might also have starred in a theatrical *The Wizard of Oz:* At the end, the Scarecrow could get Close's brain and the Tin Man his heart. Speaking of hearts . . .

06 Your Beatin' Heart

After Percy Bysshe Shelley drowned while sailing in 1822 (see p. 208), his body was cremated on the beach with fellow Romantic poet Lord Byron looking on. Shelley's heart, however, refused to burn—at least according to Lord Byron, who admittedly was the Pinocchio of British Romantic poetry. So while Shelley's cremains* were buried in the Protestant cemetery in Rome, his heart was given to his wife, Mary (of *Frankenstein* fame), who wrapped it in a copy of a poem Shelley had written—and promptly stuck it in a drawer. That's pretty unsentimental on the one hand, but on the other: What are you going to do with your dead husband's unburnable heart anyway? Take it out and pet it? Wrap it in a new poem every year? So basically it remained in storage until Mary Shelley's death almost 30 years later. Eventually, however, it was buried in Dorset, England.

✖ ✖ ✖

Lance Armstrong's resting heart rate of 40 beats per minute is pretty impressive, but Lance's heart is hardly the slowest beating on earth. That distinction goes to the happiest of clams, which have a resting heart rate of about 2 bpm.

✖ ✖ ✖

Worth bearing in mind if you're stocking a fallout shelter: NECCO's classic Valentine's Day candy hearts stay edible for about five years. (Which, incidentally, makes them a far better choice than Twinkies. Despite what you may have heard, Twinkies get rotten and moldy within a couple months.) If you're like us, you've always thought that all NECCO hearts

---

* Note: We have been waiting our entire lives to use *cremains* in a sentence.

taste like the exact same variety of sugared chalk, but it turns out that each color (supposedly) has a different flavor:

Pink → Cherry
Yellow → Banana
Orange → Orange
Green → Lemon
Purple → Grape
White → Wintergreen

✻ ✻ ✻

In the average lifetime, the human heart beats around three billion times.

HEART-SHAPED BOX

So why don't most heart-shaped boxes look like this one? Some have theorized that with its single cleft, the traditional heart shape has more to do with humanity's fascination with female buttocks than blood-pumping organs. But we prefer the theory that, for many centuries, few people in the Western world really *knew* very much about the appearance of the human heart, because looking at corpses was verboten.

✖ ✖ ✖

Leonardo da Vinci was among those who violated the Catholic Church's ban on examining the interior of bodies. He was obsessed with the human heart and its function for much of his life, and several of his intricate sketches of the heart survive. But Leonardo never figured out that the heart pumped blood, nor did his accurate drawings change the way we think of a heart shape. Perhaps that's why his last words are said to have been "I have offended God and man because my work was not good enough." Speaking of last words . . .

07 Fond Farewells:
The Best and Worst of Famous People's Last Words

399 BCE: For a guy who was put to death for his purported impiety, the Greek philosopher Socrates remains religious to the end. "Crito," he says just before drinking hemlock, "I owe a cock to Asclepius; will you remember to pay the debt?" (Asclepius was the god of healing.)

32 CE (APPROX.): Jesus dies. His last words are recorded variously as "My God, my God, why have you forsaken me?" (Mark and Matthew) or "It is finished" (John) or "Father, into your hands I commend my spirit" (Luke).

1635: Informed that he is near death, Spanish playwright Lope Félix de Vega Carpio makes a confession: "All right, then. I'll say it: Dante makes me sick."

1793: Marie "Let them eat cake" Antoinette is guillotined. Marie *intends* her last words to be "Farewell, my children, forever. I go to your father." But then she steps on her executioner's foot—so her *actual* last words are, "Monsieur, I beg your pardon."

1864: Union general John Sedgwick steps over the battle parapets during a lull in fighting. When another officer says it might not be safe, Sedgwick confidently retorts, "They couldn't hit an elephant at this dist—"

APRIL 14, 1865: Abraham Lincoln leans over to hold his wife's hand. Mary pulls away, embarrassed, and says, "What will people think?" Abe answers, "They won't think anything of it." Twelve days later, John Wilkes Booth is caught and shot, whereupon he speaks his own last words—reported to have been the apropos "Useless! Useless!"

1886: With her trademark elegance and ambiguity, Emily Dickinson says, "I must go in, the fog is rising."

1900: The great playwright Oscar Wilde (full name: Oscar Fingal O'Flahertie Wills Wilde) is dying in a garishly decorated hotel room. With his last measure of strength, he turns to a companion and says, "Either this wallpaper goes—or I do."

1906: After his nurse notes that he seems to be feeling much better, Norwegian playwright Henrik Ibsen replies, "On the contrary," and dies.

1923: Pancho Villa is assassinated in Parral, Mexico. "Don't let it end like this," he says in parting. "Tell them I said something." Let that be a lesson: It's never too early to prepare your last words.

1955: The poet Paul Claudel dies just after uttering the memorable question, "Doctor, do you think it could have been the sausage?"

1993: Murderer Thomas J. Grasso, who asked to be sentenced to death, gets his wish. But he doesn't get his last wish: "I did not get my SpaghettiOs. I got spaghetti. I want the press to know this!"

✖ ✖ ✖

Grasso, incidentally, grew up in Tulsa, Oklahoma, which was the site of the greatest Putt-Putt round ever played. Professional putter (there are such things) Daryl Freeman once went 95 under par in a two-day tournament there in 1973, acing two-thirds of the holes. Speaking of which . . .

08 Really Unbreakable Records:
The Sports Edition

BASEBALL

The Record: 54 wins by a pitcher in a season

The Record Holder: Al Spalding, Boston Braves, 1875

It's Unbreakable Because: Pitchers never even *play* 54 games a season anymore. These days, major-league baseball teams rotate at least four starting pitchers so hard-throwing arms have time to rest.

✖ ✖ ✖

The Record: 868 home runs in a professional baseball career

The Record Holder: Sadaharu Oh

It's Unbreakable Because: It's a lot. Sadaharu Oh was the Barry Bonds of Japanese professional baseball—he was never terribly well liked (due largely to the fact that he was partly of Chinese origin), but during a 21-year career that ended in 1980, Oh hit 113 more home runs than Hank Aaron, America's home-run king since 1974.

STOCK CAR RACING

The Record: 200 NASCAR victories

The Record Holder: Richard Petty, retired 1989

It's Unbreakable Because: No one's ever even gotten half-way there. These days, if one driver started dominating the way Petty did, the National Association for Stock Car Auto Racing would just change the rules and make him drive with a hand tied behind his back. (No one's ever done *that*, but retired NASCAR driver Dick Trickle, whose name we really enjoy getting into print, did reportedly smoke cigarettes during his races.)

GOLF

The Record: 11 straight PGA Tour victories

The Record Holder: Byron Nelson, 1945

It's Unbreakable Because: Very few professional golfers even *play* 11 straight events anymore, let alone win them. It was an astounding achievement when Tiger Woods won six consecutive PGA Tour tournaments, but he barely got half-way to Nelson's record.

FOOTBALL

The Record: a margin of victory of 222–0

The Record Holder: Georgia Tech had the 222, Cumberland the 0.

It's Unbreakable Because: To improve on Georgia Tech's 1916 record, a team would have to score a touchdown approximately every 1 minute and 52 seconds.

BASKETBALL

The Record: Scoring 100 points in a single game/sleeping with 20,000 women

The Record Holder: Wilt Chamberlain (scored 100 points on March 2, 1962)

It's Unbreakable Because: Wilt was one of the few seven-footers in the National Basketball Association during his career, and the rules favored him (the shooting lane was later narrowed to stop Wilt from dominating). Even so, we'll allow for the possibility somebody might one day score more than 100 points in an NBA game—but no way will that somebody have slept with 20,000 women, as Wilt claims to have done.

BADMINTON

The Record: winning 504 consecutive badminton games

The Record Holder: Miller Place (N.Y.) High School Panthers

It's Unbreakable Because: Well, for starters, very few high schools will *ever* win, or for that matter participate in, 504 games of badminton. Also, the Panthers went 32 years without a loss. No matter what sport you play, that's impressive.

SPITTING WATERMELON SEEDS

The Record: spitting a watermelon seed 66 feet, 11 inches

The Record Holder: Jack Die—wait, what's that you say? Spitting watermelon seeds isn't a *sport*? Well, sure, but neither is badminton—and you weren't complaining a minute ago. But okay. Fine. If watermelon seed spitting isn't a sport . . .

09 Really Unbreakable Records:
The Nonsports Edition

. . . then we'll just mention it here:

The Record: spitting a watermelon seed 66 feet, 11 inches

The Record Holder: Jack Dietz of Chicago

Why It's Unbreakable: Watermelon seeds ain't what they used to be. Genetic engineering has begun to take a toll on the quality of watermelon seed spits. Because seedless watermelons have crossbred with seeded ones, watermelon seeds "just don't have the mass" they used to, to quote Mr. Dietz himself. A lighter, smaller seed means more wind resistance, making Dietz's record safe to history.

✹ ✹ ✹

The Record: eating 1,000 oysters in a single day (according to Roman historians)

The Record Holder: Vitellius, who was Emperor of Rome for all of about three weeks

It's Unbreakable Because: Have you seen what they're charging for oysters these days? Only a Roman emperor could afford 1,000 oysters, let alone eat them.

It's interesting to note that while Vitellius constantly indulged his own gluttony, he purportedly starved his mother to death to fulfill a (manifestly false) prophecy that his reign would only be long if he outlived his parents.

✹ ✹ ✹

The Record: Eating a bicycle. 18 bicycles, actually. Also a cash register, a coffin, 15 shopping carts, and an entire airplane

The Record Holder: Michel Lotito, who has eaten about two pounds of ground-up metal every day since 1959

It's Unbreakable Because: Well, first, because *Guinness World Records* won't allow any challengers, due to health risks. And second, because—um, are *you* going to eat 18 bicycles? Even Monsieur Lotito, whose gastrointestinal system is—pardon the pun—made of steel, finds it difficult to eat all that Plexiglas, rubber, and real glass. "Rubber," he has noted, "tastes horrible." We'll take his word on it.

✖ ✖ ✖

The Record: the same painting getting stolen four separate times

The Record Holder: Rembrandt's *Jacob III de Gheyn* (1632)

It's Unbreakable Because: Jacob III de Gheyn is uniquely susceptible to theft because 1) Rembrandt is a very famous artist, and 2) the painting is small enough to fit in a pants pocket. Known as the "takeaway Rembrandt," the portrait is now housed in a London museum under extraordinary security—so don't get any ideas.

✖ ✖ ✖

The Record: longest period between proposals of paradoxes and their solution

The Record Holder: Georg Cantor, who helped explain Zeno's Achilles paradox 2,500 years after Zeno thought it up

It's Unbreakable Because: There aren't a lot of theoretically solvable ancient math quandaries left unsolved. Zeno's paradox states that, like, you can never walk *through* a door because first you have to go halfway to the door, and then halfway again, ad infinitum. Mostly, people kept walking through doors and not worrying about this until Georg Cantor figured out the solution. Speaking of whom . . .

10 Math Nerds Gone Wild
(And by Wild, We Mean Nuts)

Georg Cantor's (1845–1918) brilliance is such that other mathematicians talk about him in reverent, almost mystical tones. The German mathematician David Hilbert (1862–1943) once said, "No one shall expel us from the Paradise that Cantor has created." We'd try to explain that paradise, except we don't even remotely understand it. Cantor basically invented set theory, which allowed him to solve Zeno's aforementioned Achilles paradox by proving that some infinities are—get this—bigger than other infinities. (Ergo, we are able to walk through a door because all the infinities involved in getting halfway to the door are, relatively speaking, small.) Such massively abstract thinking can make you feel a little bonkers, and Cantor was no exception—he suffered several nervous breakdowns and spent the last years of his life trying to prove that God was a kind of infinite number and that Francis Bacon wrote Shakespeare's plays.

✹ ✹ ✹

Although he lives in hiding and communicates only via occasional, thousands-of-pages-long letters to colleagues, Alexandre Grothendieck is widely considered one of the most important mathematicians of the 20th century. A radical environmentalist and Communist, Grothendieck has, since the 1980s, communicated his mathematical concepts primarily in very long, handwritten letters that circulate among mathematicians. The 1,600-page *Long Walk Through Galois Theory,* for instance, doesn't strike us as a very compelling beach read, but Grothendieck's colleagues have been poring over it for 25 years.

✖ ✖ ✖

In his 30s, British engineer and mathematician Oliver Heaviside (1850–1925) made important discoveries in how to transform differential equations into relatively simple algebra, a discovery that had a profound impact on the lives of advanced calculus students and absolutely no one else. In the last decades of his life, Heaviside's lifelong eccentricity morphed into madness. He started painting his fingernails pink—which while perfectly acceptable now was weird in the 1920s—and he moved all the furniture out of his house, replacing everything with granite blocks of varying sizes.

✖ ✖ ✖

Shortly after the publication of his book on nonlinear functions in 1996, Ukrainian-American mathematician Walter Petryshyn discovered the book contained an error. Terrified that he would be the laughingstock of the nonlinear function community, he went mad—in both senses of the word. His depression and paranoia culminated with the murder of his wife. All of which just goes to prove what we told our parents when they saw our grades in calculus: Chill out, man. It's just *math*.

✖ ✖ ✖

One of the inarguable facts of the human condition is that mathematicians, as a class, do not excel at dueling (see Tycho Brahe, p. 228). But apparently no one ever told this to Evariste Galois, the 19th-century Frenchman whose contributions to algebra got a theory named after him. Galois didn't live to see himself get famous, though, because he died in a duel at the ripe old age of 20. Here's the crazy part, though: Some believe that Galois *staged* the duel to look like a police ambush, in hopes that his death might incite a democratic revolution. (Talk about delusions of grandeur.) Mathematicians were awfully political back then. For example, Galois's former mentor, Joseph "Numbers" Fourier, traveled to Egypt with an influential fellow by the name of . . .

II Napoléon Bonaparte

Let's clear this up once and for all: Napoléon could not possibly have had a "Napoléon complex," at least not in the classical sense of the phrase, because he wasn't short. He was 5'6½", making him an inch and a half taller than the average European of his day.

✼ ✼ ✼

There may be other reasons why they called him the "Little Corporal." It seems likely that the priest present during Napoléon's autopsy made off with the Little Corporal's Little Corporal, if you catch our drift. This relic of Napoléon has changed hands several times and is now owned by an American urologist. But to answer your question: When the item was put on display in the late 1920s, newspaper reports said it was an inch long and compared it to a "shriveled eel."

✼ ✼ ✼

Things didn't go terribly well for Napoléon's descendants, either. His only son died, apparently of heart failure, at 21. Napoléon III, who was actually Napoléon's nephew, not his grandson, managed to become Emperor of France—but he died in exile after losing the Franco-Prussian War. But the worst was yet to come: Napoléon's last name-bearing descendant, Jerome Napoleon Bonaparte, died after tripping over his dog's leash in 1945. Napoléon himself was not afraid of dogs—but he did suffer from ailurophobia, the morbid fear of cats.

Napoléon's Dynamite!
MY RÉSUMÉ, BY NAPOLÉON BONAPARTE

EXPERIENCE

1821–present **Dead Person**
The Afterlife
- Nephew, Napoléon III, used name to become Emperor of France
- Era ("The Napoleonic") named after me
- Traveled through time and became fond of ice cream in *Bill and Ted's Excellent Adventure*

1815–1821 **Emperor-in-Exile**
St. Helena, in the South Atlantic
- Dictated memoirs
- Tried (with very limited success) to learn English
- Died (1821), possibly of arsenic poisoning

1814–1815 **Emperor of Elba/France**
Elba Island, off the Italian Coast
- Escaped from exile
- Turned the French army from the king, retook rightful throne, raised an army of 200,000
- Attacked the European allied army at Waterloo. Whoops. 34,000 French casualties.

1799–1814   **Leader/First Consul Emperor of France and KING OF THE WORLD!**
Wherever there were . . . battles to fight

- Took control of France after tumultuous decade of the French Revolution
- Improved everything from sewage to education systems, built roads, and ushered in modern European legal system with the Napoleonic Code
- Fought the Prussians, the British, the Italians, the Dutch, the Egyptians, the Russians, and pretty much anyone else who didn't welcome Napoleonic rule
- On the upside: Won most battles and established the largest French Empire *ever*
- On the downside: Responsible for the death of approximately six million people; eventual loss permanently hurt France's standing in Europe

EDUCATION

1784–1786   **École Royale Militaire**

- Studied artillery, which later came in handy. Became famous in 1795 for using artillery to repel royalist attackers on the streets of Paris.

PERSONAL

Married great love of life, Joséphine, in 1796. Had marriage with great love of life annulled in 1810 because she didn't seem capable of bearing male heirs. If only empresses had babies in litters . . .

6

01 Puppies

Before puppy love (the kind that human teenagers experience) was called puppy love (the first recorded use was in 1834), it was known as "calf love." Equally immature but somehow less adorable. In fact, the language of love is always changing. Why, it wasn't too long ago that "flirting" with a "hunk" for example, meant something entirely different than it does today. The word *hunk* used to refer to a slow-witted or fat man, and the verb *to flirt* originally meant "to snub."

✖ ✖ ✖

About dog years: The seven-human-years-per-dog-year formula for determining a dog's age isn't the best available. The first year of a puppy's life is equal to about 21

Taking the Bull Out of the Bulldog

Bulldogs are so named not because they look like bulls (which, you'll note, they don't), but rather because they were bred for the exclusive purpose of attacking bulls. In the spectator sport of "bull baiting," which dates to the Middle Ages, a bulldog would bite into a bull's nose and then hang on while the bull bucked and attempted to gore the dog. (This is still done today, but now, with humans, and it's called "rodeo.") For this reason, owners bred dogs with short teeth (so they wouldn't hurt the bull *too* badly), squat bodies (harder for bulls to gore), and a turned-up nose (so they could still breathe even while latched onto a bull). Altogether brilliant breeding, except for one problem: The bodies of bulldogs don't actually lend themselves to breeding. They've been so selectively bred that generally bulldogs can no longer do it themselves—so most bulldog pups are the product of artificial insemination.

human years; every succeeding year is equal to about four human years.

✖ ✖ ✖

Just like many human babies, puppies are often born with blue eyes that darken in the first few months of their lives.

✖ ✖ ✖

As for when it's safe to neuter or spay your puppy: Puppies are generally spayed or neutered between the ages of five and eight months, but recent studies have shown that the operations are safe in dogs as young as six weeks. And just so you know, some puppies begin humping legs at the tender age of four weeks. (They aren't sexually mature for several months, but it's never too early to start practicing!)

The Scoop on Poop

It's an ancient question: Why do puppies, um, eat their poop? There's a name for that phenomenon, incidentally—coprophagia, which we'll use because it sounds less disgusting than the alternatives. Some veterinary scientists believe that puppies engage in coprophagia due to mineral deficiencies and that giving dogs a multivitamin will address the issue. Others argue that it's a result of owners using the old "rub their nose in it" potty-training strategy.

By doing this, some say, you're basically teaching your puppy the secret joys of coprophagia. But thus far, no one has definitively discovered the biology behind the phenomenon, which we think is just, well, crappy. Honestly, we can send a dog into space but we can't convince him not to indulge in eating his feces? Oh, and yes—we *can* send a dog into space . . .

02 Pets Around (and Occasionally Out of) This World

RUSSIA (ALSO OUTER SPACE): In 1957, a stray dog from the streets of Moscow became the first dog in space—proving that dogs *always* can be tricked into going for a ride, no matter how far. The mission also proved that yes, dogs can live in space, and yes, dogs can die in space . . . especially when they don't have any food or oxygen. Laika (known to Americans as Muttnik) was cremated upon reentry 163 days after launch.

✖ ✖ ✖

WASHINGTON, D.C.: The White House saw raccoons roaming the halls under Calvin Coolidge; Teddy Roosevelt's son's pony took a ride in a White House elevator; Benjamin Harrison's presidential goat, Old Whiskers, escaped and had to be chased down Pennsylvania Avenue; and Warren Harding's Airedale terrier sat in on cabinet meetings. Apparently, it's not easy to find human friends when you're the president. Harry Truman summed it up: "If you want to find a friend in Washington," he once said, "get a dog."

✖ ✖ ✖

PEOPLE'S REPUBLIC OF CHINA: In the 1960s and '70s Mao Zedong decided that dogs (even dogs being raised as livestock) were filthy manifestations of bourgeois decadence and had them all killed, proving once again that anyone carrying pictures of Chairman Mao ain't gonna make it with anyone anyhow. But now, 30 years later, the Chinese taboo on pets is slowly lifting. In a country where Big Brother says you can only have one child, these days he'll let you have several dogs.

✖ ✖ ✖

GERMANY: Even Hitler had a dog. Blondi was a German (surprise!) shepherd who slept by Hitler's bed every night in his Berlin bunker and probably gave an evil man pure and unconditional love. In return for this service, Hitler let her have a cyanide tablet right before he and Eva Braun ate their own.

✖ ✖ ✖

THE HIGH SEAS: Animals aboard pirate ships may have been well loved, but hard life on the high seas trumps love. Whole swaths of the Earth's oceans were dubbed Horse Lattitudes, where winds stopped blowing and horses were slaughtered and consumed. As for parrots, they were kept in cages and used to bribe port officials in the 18th century because their feathers carried considerable value. Oh, and the bird on Long John Silver's shoulder? It was an invention of author Robert Louis Stevenson and would probably have created an unacceptable mess for an actual swashbuckler.

✖ ✖ ✖

THE EVERGLADES: Pet Burmese pythons have long been "set free" in Florida's Everglades after reaching unmanageable lengths, and the python population in the Everglades now seems to be self-sustaining. If you fear pythons (and who doesn't?), the man to ask for intercession is Saint Patrick. The patron saint of Ireland is also the man some believe

responsible for having thus far kept Ireland a snake-free isle.
All of which brings us to . . .

03 Patron Saints

What You've Got: a lost cause

Whom You Need: The problem with Saint Jude Thaddeus is
that he was also known as "Judas Jacobi, the most forgettable
disciple," which sounds a lot like "Judas Iscariot, the guy who
betrayed Jesus." Both were disciples, but J.T. did *not* betray J.C.
for 30 lousy pieces of silver. Early Christians didn't understand
that the slight difference in name represented a large difference in piousness, and thus devotion to Saint Jude became a
hopeless cause, making Jude the patron saint of lost causes.
And while he may have gotten no love in the first couple centuries of the Common Era, Jude has made a remarkable comeback. Besides being regularly thanked in newspaper classified
ads throughout the world, the saint of last resort has also been
the subject of two recent biographies.

✖ ✖ ✖

What You've Got: hemorrhoids

Whom You Need: Saint Fiacre, a seventh-century Irish
monk renowned for his power to heal people by laying his
hands on them. Of course, this makes us loath to imagine
how and why he came to be the patron saint of hemorrhoids.
But Fiacre was something of a misogynist. He never allowed
women into his hermitage or his chapel, and it's said that
centuries after his death, in 1620, a woman from Paris was
driven mad after entering into his sacred space. Whether or

not she was seeking a cure for hemorrhoids is not a matter of historical record.

✖ ✖ ✖

What You Want: a six-pack (we're talking brewskis, not abs!)

Whom You Need: Sadly, there is no actual patron saint of beer (although there are some apocryphal ones). There are, however, no fewer than *12* patron saints of brewers, including Saint Nicholas of Myra, who is more commonly known as—that's right—Santa Claus. The story goes that Old Saint Nick, a fourth-century bishop in Myra, Lycia (now known as Turkey), resurrected three clerics who had been slain at an inn that doubled as a brewery. When he's not busy tallying up whether children have been naughty or nice, Saint Nick enjoys serving as the patron saint of fishermen, Greece, and spinsters, among others.

✖ ✖ ✖

What You Want: a new television

Whom You Need: A friend of Saint Francis, Saint Clare of Assisi founded the Order of the Poor Ladies, the feminine companion to the Franciscan Order. But, like most people in the 13th century, Clare did not own a television. At the end of her life, though, when she was too sick to attend mass, images of the mass would miraculously appear on her wall like a heavenly flat screen. Miracles like this made for a very quick canonization for Clare. Just two years after her death in 1253 (exactly 700 years before the first color TV broadcast), Pope Alexander IV made her a saint.

✖ ✖ ✖

What You Want: a pet pig

Whom You Need: The patron saint of pigs is Saint Anthony of Egypt (251–356), who's most famous for his healings. So how'd he get linked up with the porksters? Well, mainly because of his ham-made cures. Back in Anthony's day skin disease was often treated with the application of pork fat. Therefore, Anthony was often painted with pigs in tow, and worshippers came to see him as a pig-friendly saint (although there's no record he ever hung out with live ones). Speaking of pigs, though . . .

04 Battles Royal:
The Other White Meat

MISS PIGGY VERSUS BOSS HOGG

Blue Corner: Miss Piggy, puppet diva extraordinaire, leading lady of *The Muppet Show* (1976–1981). Violent and unpredictable, she practices her moves regularly by sparring with a lovable frog.

Red Corner: Boss Hogg, redneck kingpin nonpareil (who was played by a Shakespearean actor wearing a fat suit). Chief antagonist of *The Dukes of Hazzard* (1979–1985).

The Feud: The small screen just ain't big enough for the two of 'em—in every sense.

The Breakdown: Neither fighter is conditioned to go the distance, so this one'll be decided in the first few rounds. Count on Hogg to bribe the ref with moonshine money and stick to the ropes. If Piggy can land her famed karate chop, though, it'll be lights out for the boss.

The Victor: Miss Piggy, *mais oui.* Don't mess with the pig, Bub.

WILBUR VERSUS NAPOLEON

Blue Corner: Wilbur, lovable hero of E. B. White's classic *Charlotte's Web*

Red Corner: Napoleon, despicable despot of George Orwell's classic *Animal Farm,* who rules with paranoia and unchallenged authority over a farm bearing a suspicious resemblance to postrevolutionary Russia

The Feud: What should pigs wear—clothes or mud? Which is stronger—innocence or cynicism? Whose prose style is crisper—Orwell's or White's?

The Breakdown: Like most dictators and bullies, Napoleon isn't at his best one on one. Also, his newly developed smoking habit will likely have an adverse effect on late-round performance. Wilbur, though, is gentle, trusting, and not that bright. Expect Napoleon to attempt to con him into conceding with his seductive socialistic Seven Commandments of Animalism, particularly the one about animals not killing each other.

The Victor: Napoleon. Alas, to quote the last commandment after revision by the pigs: "All animals are equal, but some are more equal than others."

SWINE FLU VERSUS TRICHINOSIS

Blue Corner: swine flu. Vicious virus. The swine flu virus, carried mainly by birds, caused the devastating 1918 "Spanish flu" pandemic. Kills quickly by obstructing the lungs, causing bodily fluid drowning and, occasionally, fatal malnourishment.

Red Corner: trichinosis. Parasite that thrives in undercooked pork and game. Kills through attrition, gradually weakening its victim with fever and chronic diarrhea. Transferred through undercooked meat.

The Feud: Swine flu used to be the baddest porcine plague on the block, but a 1976 false scare by the Ford Administration turned it into a laughingstock. Now this legendary ex-champ wants a comeback shot against the slow but steady trichina worm.

The Breakdown: Swine flu hasn't been in the game for a while, but it hasn't lost any of the old punching power. Trichinosis can only hope its mere 38 or so U.S. cases a year will be enough to squeak by on a split decision.

The Victor: swine flu, no contest. The way to trichinosis's glass chin is common knowledge: Simply cook the pork. Swine flu, on the other hand, is a consistently surprising fighter, often leaving doctors baffled about prevention. In 1918, for example, the best many of them could come up with was "consume more alcohol," giving a war-weary Europe, and American soldiers like Papa Hemingway, another excuse to hit the cafés.

05 Alcoholism in Literature
(Drunk Writers)

SHERWOOD ANDERSON

The Man: A thrice-divorced workaholic, Anderson used heavy drink to force himself to relax, and to further irritate his various long-suffering wives. His father, also a drunk, though a conspicuously lazy one, served as both model and cautionary example.

His Work: the revered short story collection *Winesburg, Ohio*, which is not about wine, but which does feature a number of characters who, in their existential loneliness and small-town angst, sure seem like they could use a drink. Indeed, one story is entitled "Drink," though the lead character only gets intoxicated one time and doesn't seem to enjoy it much. Anderson also produced a number of rather less-revered novels and stories, including one called "The Triumph of the Egg," which really is about an egg.

His Drink: dry classic gin martini with olives

His Death: Partying aboard an ocean liner bound for Brazil, Anderson swallowed part of a toothpick, either from an hors d'oeuvre or his ubiquitous cocktail, and promptly developed an acute case of peritonitis.

DOROTHY PARKER

The Woman: The bitter belle of the Algonquin Round Table, Parker set the pace for a truly world-class assemblage of drunks, who whiled away each afternoon getting pickled at Manhattan's Algonquin Hotel and making savage remarks about anyone unfortunate enough not to have been invited. Inordinately fond of highly dysfunctional love affairs, Parker coined the immortal, often alcohol-related phrase "one-night stand."

Her Work: darkly humorous poems, witty stories, and occasional vicious literary reviews, including a memorable attack on *Winnie-the-Pooh*

Her Drink: martini, but make hers with a twist. And she'll have four of them, as per her famous line "Three and I'm under the table, four and I'm under the host."

Her Death: Despite her unhealthy habits, which included four suicide attempts, she died of a heart attack at the ripe old age of 73. Since she had no next of kin, her ashes wound up spending 15 years in her lawyer's filing cabinet.

DYLAN THOMAS

The Man: Welsh poetical superstar who once said, "An alcoholic is someone you don't like who drinks as much as you."

His Work: some of the 20th century's greatest, most powerfully lyrical poems. Also a terrific play, *Under Milk Wood*.

His Drink and Death: whiskey. Thomas's apocryphal record is 18 straight, which, according to legend, is also the binge that killed him. His last words are reported to have been, "After 39 years, this is all I've done," which may or may not have been referring to that whiskey record.

F. SCOTT FITZGERALD

The Man: along with fellow lush Ernest Hemingway, literary co-champion of the American Lost Generation. Unlike Hemingway, had low tolerance and got drunk quickly. He married Zelda, a free-spirited schizophrenic who probably would have driven him to drink even if he hadn't already been hooked.

His Work: *The Great Gatsby*. Several other novels, loads of short stories, and some embarrassing Hollywood hackwork

His Drink: champagne cocktail

His Death: of a heart attack, while eating a Hershey bar and listening to Beethoven. His funeral was sparsely attended, but Dorothy Parker reputedly showed up in inebriate solidarity and cried, quoting the touching *Gatsby* line, "The poor son of a bitch."

16 Alcoholism in Literature
(Severely Sozzled Characters)

Abe North—*Tender Is the Night* by F. Scott Fitzgerald
Failed musician with a propensity for getting his friends caught up in dangerous trouble. Abe gets robbed at gunpoint while drunk, accuses the wrong man of the crime, and ends up bludgeoned to death in a speakeasy.

❊ ❊ ❊

Michael Henchard—*The Mayor of Casterbridge* by Thomas Hardy
"Hay-trusser" who becomes so soused he sells his wife and daughter at a country fair for five guineas. Penitent, he swears off alcohol for good and goes on to become a successful merchant and mayor of Casterbridge. Then his wife and daughter show up and ruin everything. His final wish is to be forever forgotten.

❊ ❊ ❊

The Whisky Priest—*The Power and the Glory* by Graham Greene
Nameless and deeply flawed, not just with alcoholism but also lechery and cowardice, because Greene was making a point about the inviolate nature of the holy sacraments, regardless of how contemptible the character in the robe happens to be. The priest is chased all over Mexico and eventually gets a happy ending, but only so you can also catch a glimpse of his arrogance.

❊ ❊ ❊

Pap Finn—*The Adventures of Huckleberry Finn* by Mark Twain
Regularly beats the stuffing out of one of the Western

Canon's most beloved protagonists. Ghostlike, disheveled, and typically "drunk as a fiddler," he even tries to steal Huck's reward money, which the poor kid spent the entire last third of *The Adventures of Tom Sawyer* earning.

✖ ✖ ✖

Sebastian Flyte—*Brideshead Revisited* by Evelyn Waugh

Literature's most famous lapsed Catholic. Flyte drinks either out of guilt over abandoning the church or repressed homosexuality or some combination of the two. None of this is presumably helped by the constant presence of his handsome agnostic school chum Charles, who narrates and eventually falls for Sebastian's sister. After Sebastian gets kicked out of the university, everyone gives up on him, with the lone exception of his darling stuffed teddy bear, Aloysius.

✖ ✖ ✖

Julian English—*Appointment in Samarra* by John O'Hara

Depressive, womanizing Cadillac dealer who self-destructively, and somewhat inexplicably, stumbles toward his inevitable rendezvous with death. The protagonist is almost as unlikable as John O'Hara himself, a man who spent his entire career alienating other writers and demanding a Nobel Prize. Julian commits suicide via carbon monoxide in the end, while O'Hara, despite the lack of a Nobel, passed away of natural causes, inscribing for himself the modest epitaph "Better than anyone else, he told the truth about his time."

✖ ✖ ✖

Elwood P. Dowd—*Harvey* by Mary Chase

A perfectly sane fellow with plenty of disposable inherited wealth, a fondness for midday martinis, and a best friend who happens to be a pooka, a terrifying Celtic faerie that usually takes the form of a giant black horse. In this case, though, the pooka looks like a six-foot-plus rabbit, and only Elwood can see him. Elwood utters the memorable lines, "Nobody ever brings anything small into a bar" and "I've wrestled with reality for 35 years, Doctor, and I'm happy to say I finally won out over it." Was Elwood trying to say that he lived on Fantasy Island? . . .

07 Da Plane! Da Plane!
The Best and Worst from the Annals of Aviation

BEST

Charles Lindbergh

Sure, he later became notorious as an outspoken isolationist, anti-Semite, and possible Nazi sympathizer, but the man could fly. In 1927, with the first nonstop solo flight across the Atlantic, he gained iconic American status second only to Babe Ruth. (The president, Calvin Coolidge, did not place.) Lindbergh kept himself awake and sane on the 33-hour trip by playing with a Felix the Cat doll and frequently punching himself in the face. Eventual questions of patriotism aside, Lucky Lindy was fortunate, for the purposes of posterity, that his grandfather had changed the family surname upon immigrating, or all the ticker-tape parades would have been in honor of one Charles Mannson.

BEST

The Gossamer Albatross

Essentially a flying bicycle, this person-powered plane actually made it across the English Channel in less than three hours, kept aloft by nothing but a single sweaty cyclist named Bryan Allen. With the constant rise in American obesity and the eventual depletion of the world's fossil fuels, this inspired combination of air travel and physical fitness should come in quite handy in the future. Though with its fragile structure and a total empty weight of only 70 pounds, you'd probably be wise to lose a few ounces in the gym beforehand.

WORST

The Messerschmitt Me 163

The first, and still the only, tailless rocket-powered fighter plane, was one of a kind for a variety of reasons. Most notably, this manned firework was among the Luftwaffe's last desperate gambles of World War II. Admittedly very fast, its unreliable motor was troublingly prone to explosion upon ignition, and its only method of landing, a terrifying extended skid that often flipped the plane over, was little better. Lucky pilots would come away from the experience with nothing but a nasty case of whiplash, while others would find themselves engulfed by a ball of flame. In the end, the rocket plane ultimately killed more German aviators than Allied.

BEST AND WORST

Amelia Earhart

History's greatest female pilot as well as aviation's most famous disappearing act. Early on, the press dubbed her "Lady Lindy," not just due to her prowess in the skies, but because they observed, somewhat unflatteringly, that she looked just like him. In keeping with her counterpart's somewhat spotty reputation regarding World War II, a peculiar urban legend arose that

Earhart was actually captured by the Japanese and later forced into becoming the English-fluent radio propagandist Tokyo Rose.

WORST

Douglas "Wrong Way" Corrigan

One of the men who helped to construct *The Spirit of St. Louis,* Corrigan likewise dreamed of personal aviation glory. Instead, he would become infamous for somehow misreading his instruments and flying from New York all the way to Ireland, which he apparently mistook for California. In fairness, Corrigan, who'd been repeatedly denied a transatlantic permit, probably did it on purpose, but he opted to go down in history as a spectacular bonehead rather than have his license revoked. Corrigan never did admit his intention, though he finally came clean with the embarrassing truth, 50 years later, that his real name was Clyde. An embarrassing name to be sure, but better than Ulysses Grant's, as you'll soon see. . . .

❚❚ Our Wacky Presidents

George Washington was a consistent disappointment to his mother, Mary. She complained frequently to anyone who would listen that he was lax in supporting her and, much to his embarrassment, once begged the Virginia legislature for a little spending money.

John Adams spoke with a lisp because he stubbornly refused to wear dentures.

Thomas Jefferson, despite his otherwise refined tastes, was a notoriously lousy dresser with poor posture. He once shocked a British minister with his slovenly appearance.

"Hail to the Chief" was written specifically for *James Madison,* because he was so short that no one ever noticed when he entered the room.

James Monroe was driven to the brink of bankruptcy by his spendthrift wife and daughters; Monroe's wife then compounded matters by developing an expensive, and eventually fatal, illness.

Partial to skinny-dipping in the Potomac, *J. Q. Adams* was once surprised midswim by an enterprising female reporter, who forced him into a naked interview.

Andrew Jackson made his wife, Rachel, a bigamist by illegally marrying her before she'd divorced her first husband.

Martin Van Buren liked to gamble on the outcome of elections.

William Henry Harrison was the biggest vote getter in American history if calculating by what percentage of eligible voters chose him—but was only president for 31 days.

John Tyler holds the presidential paternity record. He had 14 children live to maturity, the youngest born when Tyler was 70.

James K. Polk was plagued by diarrhea throughout his single term. He eventually died of what he described as "a derangement of the stomach and bowels."

Zachary Taylor received so much fan mail after his Mexican War victories that he started refusing all postage-due letters. As a result, he didn't find out he'd won the Whig nomination for president for almost a month.

Millard Fillmore had a historic audience with the pope shortly before being nominated for president on a violently anti-Catholic ticket.

Franklin Pierce was pals with author Nathaniel Hawthorne. In fact, the two were vacationing together in the White Mountains when Hawthorne died in his sleep.

James Buchanan had one eye set higher in his head than the other, so he walked around with his neck cocked to one side.

Abraham Lincoln had a twangy high-pitched voice—nothing at all like Sam Waterston's.

Andrew Johnson loved the circus.

Ulysses S. Grant changed his name from Hiram Ulysses because he was ashamed of the initials H.U.G. Also, he hated music. All music.

Rutherford B. Hayes was a huge fan of croquet.

James A. Garfield, a former classics teacher, could simultaneously write Greek with one hand and Latin with the other.

Chester A. Arthur had over 80 pairs of pants and insisted on changing several times a day.

Grover Cleveland had a prosthetic jaw and an illegitimate daughter, neither of which seriously affected his popularity. He's also the only president to have been elected to two nonconsecutive terms.

Benjamin Harrison had the first electric lights in the White House, but was scared to turn them on or off for fear of electrocution. Instead, he made the servants do it.

William McKinley's wife was an epileptic whose contorted face he sometimes covered up with a handkerchief during formal dinner parties.

Theodore Roosevelt's mother and first wife died on the same day, in the same house, on the fourth anniversary of his engagement, which was also Valentine's Day. Rough.

As president, *William Howard Taft* weighed 326 pounds and got stuck in the White House bathtub. He had a bigger one installed.

Woodrow Wilson was a gifted mimic fond of telling racist jokes in Irish dialect. He also liked to imitate drunks.

Warren G. Harding kept his romantic trysts in the closet—literally. He often met his mistress in a closet off the presidential office.

Calvin Coolidge, while president, enjoyed riding on a mechanical horse and whooping like a cowboy. He also thought it was great fun to hit the buzzer for the servants and then hide.

Herbert Hoover and his wife were both proficient in Chinese and would often use it to talk privately in the presence of guests.

Franklin D. Roosevelt had a collection of over 25,000 stamps. He added to it by simply having the Postmaster General and State Department mail him every new issue.

Harry S Truman once wrote a threatening letter to the music critic of the *Washington Post* in response to a negative review of his daughter's voice recital, stating "I never met you, but if I do, you'll need a new nose. . . ." His entire middle name, incidentally, was S.

Dwight D. Eisenhower hated cats. In retirement in Gettysburg, Pennsylvania, he enjoyed shooting at any that came near his house.

John F. Kennedy only watched the first halves of movies. Then he'd get bored.

Lyndon B. Johnson proposed to his wife, Lady Bird, on their first date, a breakfast, then bought her a wedding ring for $2.50.

Richard M. Nixon loved football. As president, he'd occasionally call up NFL coaches to chat and offer strategic advice.

Gerald R. Ford was originally named Leslie Lynch King Jr. after his biological father, who abandoned the family when Ford was an infant. The next time Ford saw him was 15 years later, when Leslie Sr. showed up without warning and gave the kid 25 bucks.

Jimmy Carter wrote a children's book called "The Little Baby Snoogle-Fleejer."

Ronald Reagan's 1965 personal memoir, *Where's the Rest of Me?* opens with the line, "The story begins with the closeup of a bottom."

George H.W. Bush was the first president to use any of the following words in his inaugural address: "cocaine," "bacteria," and "easygoingness."

Bill Clinton was eight years old when he was beaten up by a sheep. That was the day, according to his autobiography, that he learned that he could take a hard hit.

George W. Bush was the first sitting president to acquire an iPod and correspondingly the first to admit a weakness for Blackie & the Rodeo Kings. Speaking of which . . .

09 Rock!:
Historic Concerts You Totally Missed, Dude

Who, Where, When: The Moondog Coronation Ball (featuring the Dominoes, Tiny Grimes, and others), Cleveland Arena, March 21, 1952

If measured in terms of crowds enthused, rebellion sparked, or authorities frightened, the first-ever rock concert—assembled by Cleveland DJ Alan "Moondog" Freed, who famously popularized the phrase "rock and roll"—was an unqualified success. If judged, conversely, by its ability to host music and not be cancelled, the ball was kind of square. Nobody knows if it was a matter of overzealous youths crashing the gates or simply an overzealous Freed forgetting to count how many tickets he'd hawked, but with concertgoers numbering twice the arena's capacity of ten thousand, the fire marshal dropped the ball before openers Paul Williams and the Hucklebuckers closed their first number. Decades later, *Life* magazine would dub Freed's folly the birth of rock.

✳ ✳ ✳

Who, Where, When: Bob Dylan at the Newport Folk Festival, Newport, Rhode Island, July 1965

Mere moments into this mythical early performance, 24-year-old troubadour Bob Dylan brought folk fans to their feet. Bad news was, most of them were heckling, hissing, or hightailing it out of there. What had so enraged these otherwise peacenik Peters, Pauls, and Marys? Most famously, it was Dylan's 11th-hour decision to round up a rock band and go electric. Beyond just the ruckus, though, what really raised those hippies' hackles was the philosophy behind it. Folk music aimed to galvanize the masses with a message; electric rock, as far as the crowd was concerned, was sound and fury signifying nothing. Alas, Dylan had made his choice and his set lasted three songs before getting tangled up in boos. Contrary to the criticism of the day, critics regard the night at Newport as a kind of rock-and-roll bar mitzvah for Dylan, where the diminutive, quietly indignant boy wonder stepped into a persona decidedly larger—in not only sound, but also theatricality, literary scope, and cultural relevance.

✖ ✖ ✖

Who, Where, When: Elton John, Russia, 1979

During the Cold War, about the last thing that the Western world would've lent to its Russkie rivals was a rocket. Odd, then, that the first Western pop star lent to Russian audiences was the Rocket Man. As part of his 1979 comeback tour (partially in response to slumping sales following his "retirement" from live performances a distant two years previous), Elton John and percussionist Ray Cooper sashayed through the Iron Curtain to play a handful of dates around the U.S.S.R. Red audiences were tickled pink by their first encounter with Western rock decadence—but the Old Guard was surely spinning in their graves. Elton isn't much of a proletarian, after all. . . .

10 Stalin

(a.k.a. The Original Man of Steel)

The Basics: Joseph Stalin is stirring proof that if you get into an organization at its very beginning, you can rise to great prominence even if you happen to be an evil, tyrannical murderer whom no one ever liked. Stalin became a Marxist in the late 19th century, and although Lenin mentored him for a long time, he grew to mistrust him, and other Communists thought he was crazy. But Stalin managed to hang around the circles of power. After Lenin's death, he muscled Leon Trotsky and others out and took the reins himself. He went on to consolidate his power in the late 1930s by killing everyone who'd ever said or thought anything vaguely negative about him. Unfortunately, he also threw the country into a disastrous famine with his farm collectivization projects, and he sent millions to Soviet concentration camps known as *gulags*. In short, he was pretty horrible.

Joseph Stalin, Man of God

Before he was an atheistic tyrant, Josef Stalin was, oddly enough, a seminarian. He studied at a Georgian Orthodox seminary in Tiflis for five years, between 1894 and 1899. He left the seminary either because of poor health (his mom's story) or revolutionary activity (Stalin's story). Either way, Stalin clearly didn't take much of what he learned to heart. That is, assuming he had one.

✳ ✳ ✳

Although he took great pains to hide it, Stalin was not, technically, Russian. Born in Gori, Georgia (which later had the plea-

World's Worst Dad

Nikita Khrushchev wrote that Stalin loved his daughter, Svetlana, like a cat loves a mouse. And Stalin's other two kids didn't even fare *that* well. He mostly ignored his son Vasily, an alcoholic with a sadistic streak. Stalin's other boy, Yakov, was driven to shoot himself by his father's relentless cruelty. When he learned that Yakov had only been wounded, Stalin said, "Ha! He can't even shoot straight."

sure of having its population decimated by Stalin's disastrous economic policies), Stalin was christened with the distinctly un-Russian last name Dzhugashvili. ("Stalin" was a nickname derived from the Russian word for steel.) In fact, throughout his life, Stalin spoke with a thick Georgian accent. Mentioning his accent, however, was verboten in government circles.

✖ ✖ ✖

Also, you were well advised not to ridicule that famous Stalin 'stache. In a poem intended only for friends, Osip Mandelstam compared Stalin's mustache to a cockroach. Thereafter, Mandelstam was repeatedly arrested and sent to a series of those infamous gulags.

✖ ✖ ✖

In August 1941, Stalin announced that the government would arrest the families of all captured Russian officers because only "malicious traitors" would get captured by the Germans anyway. But then Yakov got captured, putting Stalin in the awkward position of technically being required to arrest himself. (Instead, he arrested Yakov's wife.) When the Germans offered a prisoner exchange, Stalin told them, "I have no son Yakov," which Yakov no doubt wished was true. Shortly thereafter, Yakov was shot and killed while running for the prison fence.

✖ ✖ ✖

Stalin once famously said, "One death is a tragedy; a million deaths is a statistic." Well, then, the statistics are staggering: Some historians believe that between the murder, the state-sanctioned famine, and the concentration camps, Stalin was responsible for 40 million deaths. Forty million people is, approximately, the population of Spain. Almost every war had a smaller death toll than that—even really, really long ones, like . . .

7

01 The Hundred Years' War:

A Year-by-Year Account, Minus the Years We Didn't Have Room For

1337: The English, based on legal technicalities and a large occupying force, were of the opinion that they owned a vast and profitable region in southwest France called Gascony. France, however, thought it owned Gascony, based on the fact that it was full of French people. The English royals pointed out that they were more or less French themselves, being descended from William the Conqueror of Normandy, and that, after closer inspection, they should own not just a part of France, but the whole darn thing. And thus was it on.

Technically a prolonged series of little wars, the Hundred Years' War actually lasted 116 years, but with several breaks along the way.

1340: The Brits came out swinging, wiping out virtually the entire French navy at the Battle of Sluys in one day. If France had planned on invading England, they'd either have to swim there or wait for someone to invent a Chunnel.

1346: Once again, England came through when it counted most, this time versus the considerably larger French army at the Battle of Crecy, thanks to their timely unveiling of the longbow. The French, quite literally, didn't know what had hit them.

1348–55: France continued to get generally stomped for the better part of a decade, with occasional intermissions for pesky distractions like the Black Plague. Meanwhile, the whole not-having-a-navy thing was really starting to get on France's nerves.

1356: Another day, another French loss, this time at the Battle of Poitiers—except this time it resulted in the capture of France's King John II.

1360: The Treaty of Brétigny was signed, giving England its precious Normandy and thus finally bringing an end to mercilessly long Twenty-three Years' War. Oh, wait . . .

1370–1400: Nine years later, it was back to square one: Now the French decided they wanted Aquitaine back, and this time behind their new king, Charles V, they actually had a plan. Charles purchased a new naval fleet and implemented more experienced generals. Oddly enough, they started to win.

1422–1453: Ah, but you can never count out the French. At least not in this one anomalous instance. Just when all appeared lost, they rallied, thanks to a boost from a teenage girl named Joan with near miraculous militaristic talents and a little invention called the cannon. The cannon helped, but in the end, we still think it was Joan of Arc who made the difference. After all, hell hath no fury like a religious canon, or cannon, we're not really sure which. Either way, though, Joan's just one of the many fierce women you simply don't want to mess with, leading us to . . .

02 Women Who Ruled

Boudicca (c. 30–62 CE), warrior queen of the Iceni of East Anglia, was "tall and terrible to look on" and perpetrator of countless gruesome atrocities, according to Roman historian Tacitus. But then, he might be a little biased, given that those atrocities were often perpetrated on Romans. In any case, Boudicca had more than a little motivation, given that Rome had betrayed her dead husband, stolen her kingdom, and had her publicly flogged and her daughters raped. Leading her tribe, the Iceni, she launched a full-scale revolt, burning London and other cities, and striking fear in the hearts of Roman men (70,000 of whom were slaughtered along the way). Unfortunately, her revolt was put down, whereupon Boudicca (perhaps fearing another flogging) poisoned herself.

✖ ✖ ✖

The unquestioned power behind the throne for three separate yet equally spineless Chinese emperors, the Empress Dowager Cixi (1835–1908) bent an ancient males-only monarchy to her will. The power she attained is said to have surpassed that of Queen Elizabeth and all on the basis of having been a really stellar concubine. After Cixi died, the whole country essentially fell apart, as chronicled in the Oscar-winning biopic of her unfortunate successor, bluntly titled *The Last Emperor*.

✖ ✖ ✖

Speaking of Oscar bait, nobody packs in the Academy like the Virgin Queen. From her sultry Cate Blanchett-y youth to her dour Judi Dench-ish later years, Elizabeth I was all Hollywood all the way. However, some might call her kind of overrated. Although she did defeat the Spanish Armada, it essentially sank itself thanks to lousy seamanship, and almost all her domestic decisions were made out of a desperate (if somewhat justified) fear of being deposed or assassinated. Still, she gets points for style, and she did save England from Civil War (albeit temporarily).

✳ ✳ ✳

Never much of a politically correct heroine, Isabella's leading role in the Inquisition and her sponsorship of Columbus make her seem like a thoroughly unenlightened monarch. With two genocides (the Moors and the Native Americans) on her résumé, she certainly didn't need any more bad press. But not even Isabella's death in 1504 was enough to stop her bloodthirsty legacy. Four centuries later, Spanish dictator Francisco Franco proclaimed Isabella his personal monarchical muse, adding ruthless fascism to her tarnished name.

✳ ✳ ✳

Forget Margaret Thatcher. The twentieth century's real Iron Lady was Mother Indira (Gandhi: 1917–1984). Taking a virtually ungovernable country, she made India a nuclear superpower and herself into an object of worship. Oh, she had her problems, of course, including allegations of voter fraud and an understandably unpopular birth control policy involving forced vasectomies. But as JFK would tell you, nothing wipes the slate clean like a memorable assassination, and by those standards, Indira's, committed by her own bodyguards, was a classic.

✳ ✳ ✳

The first female pharaoh. Heck, the earliest known female ruler in history. Hatshepsut's the one who started it all. And since they've never found her mummy, she may still be around somewhere. Should you bump into her, pronounce it "hat-SHEEP-suit." Which is our none-too-subtle way of getting to . . .

03 (Wolves in) Sheep Suits,
or Pretty Lousy Ideas that Seemed Pretty Great at the Time

ASBESTOS

From the Greek for "inextinguishable," asbestos has a long and mostly proud history of flame resistance and insulation. Charlemagne allegedly had an asbestos tablecloth that he would gleefully clean by tossing it in the fireplace. Incidence of lung cancer among his household staff is sadly unavailable. In later years, however, we came to learn that our old friend asbestos, now in the insulation business, had been filling our indoor air with innumerable evil little mineral shards. Some buildings in the U.S. constructed as late as 1986 contain asbestos in their ceilings, but they only pose a risk if the fibers break off into the air. Incidentally, asbestos insulation is *still* legal in Canada, partly because it is widely mined in the Canadian wilderness.

THALIDOMIDE

Pregnant women deserve a good night's sleep, not to mention relief from morning sickness. And the makers of thalidomide wanted to give it to them. They also didn't want to waste too much of those women's valuable time on boring fetal safety testing, so they conveniently skipped that part. Unfortunately, thalidomide wound up causing birth defects in about

12,000 babies worldwide. Luckily, none of those took place in the United States, all thanks to the vigilance of Dr. Frances Kelsey of the FDA who single-handedly kept the stuff off U.S. shelves. But thalidomide is proving to be an idea that once again seems at least partly good: In 1998, the FDA approved the drug to treat leprosy, and it's currently being studied as a treatment for prostate cancer.

YUGOSLAVIA

What happens when you put people who haven't gotten along for centuries, people who started World War I, people who can't even agree on an *alphabet,* and tell them they all live in one country? Well, the disgrace to automotive engineering that was the Yugo, for starters. The Serbs, Croats, Slovenes, and a dozen smaller ethnic groups were thrown together after World War I and in 1929 came to be known as the Kingdom of Yugoslavia. The kingdom spluttered along, Yugo-like, until World War II, when Hitler decided Yugoslavia belonged to him on account of how it contained about eight ethnic Germans. In 1946, the country ended up on the wrong side of the Iron Curtain and started going by the name of Socialist Federal Republic of Yugoslavia. It was ruled by dictator Josip Broz Tito until his death in 1980, after which regional representatives ruled the country. Although it never had more than 21 million people, Yugoslavia's language, religious, and cultural differences—not to mention a jerk named Milošević— made it impossible for them to get along. After the decade of fighting that followed the Soviet Bloc's breakup, what was Yugoslavia is now five separate, tiny, and comparably peaceful nations (plus semiautonomous Kosovo). That seems like a good idea at *this* time; let's just hope it lasts.

COMMUNISM

It really did sound like a nice idea. Workers of the world unite! No more violent nationalism! No shameful poverty. No racial or class distinctions. Well, right on. Unfortunately, of course, it didn't work at all, either in totalitarian regimes or '60s counterculture. Just as Orwell said, absolute power corrupts absolutely—whether it's a Wyoming commune or a Communist empire. If you don't believe us, just ask a certain former schoolteacher. . . .

04 Accidental Geniuses:
People Who Changed the World with Their Second Careers

BENITO MUSSOLINI

Original Occupation: elementary schoolteacher

Second Career: fascist dictator

Reason for Switch: tough job market

How He Changed the World: Mussolini had to work his way up to dictator, of course, but that's a lot easier than finding a teaching position that pays a living wage. Mussolini was certified as an elementary schoolmaster in 1901, but when he moved to Switzerland in search of work, he couldn't find any. It's hard to know whether to be grateful. On the one hand, no one would wish Mussolini on unsuspecting young minds, but if he'd found fulfillment in Switzerland, he might not have returned to Italy and taken a job reporting and editing for a small newspaper. After serving in World War I, he returned to editing, but his increasing activism in Italy's fascist party grew to be too much of a distraction, and he decided to become a full-time fascist. It worked out awfully well for him—within three years, he was Italy's dictator.

HENRI MATISSE

Original Occupation: lawyer/court administrator

Second Career: painter

Reason for Switch: severe appendicitis

How He Changed the World: Matisse took up painting when his slow recovery from appendicitis left him bedridden, unable to work, and bored. Within a few years he was the most prominent painter in France and was leading the Fauvist movement. In their brief heyday (1905–1908) *Les Fauves* ("the Wild Beasts") managed to shock the Parisian art world with their bold colors and sharp black outlines. Even after Fauvism ceased to impress critics, Matisse never did. Although his friend and rival Pablo Picasso is probably better known, these days Matisse paintings sell for as much as $17 million, which ain't bad. Talk about a fortuitous appendicitis eruption!

COLONEL SANDERS

Original Occupation: insurance salesman

Second Career: chicken magnate

Reason for Switch: people too healthy to worry about insurance

How He Changed the World: Frustrated by financial hardship, Sanders spent years concocting an infernal, irresistible blend of 11 herbs and spices to shorten life spans and fatten up America. Apparently, revenge is a dish best served hot, extra crispy, and finger-lickin' good.

GERALD FORD

Original Occupation: male model

Second Career: politician, congressman, U.S. president

Reason for Switch: breakup with girlfriend/longing for home

How He Changed the World: Handsome young Gerry Ford easily made the transition from all-American football star (he was once offered a contract to play for the Green Bay Packers) to model in glossy fashion spreads in the likes of *Life* and *Cosmopolitan.* But Ford disliked New York and missed his hometown, Grand Rapids, Michigan. Ford ditched the high-fashion world for the campaign trail, first getting elected a congressman in Michigan, and then managing to become president without ever being elected (he wasn't elected vice president, either—he simply replaced the disgraced Spiro Agnew). As president, Ford was bumbling and goofy—but few people hated him. And if you're president, you really don't want to have the wrong people hate you. . . .

05 Assassi-nation:

American Presidential Assassinations Through the Years

ABRAHAM LINCOLN—APRIL 14, 1865

What You Already Know: Lincoln was shot at Ford's Theatre by a deranged Southern-sympathetic actor named John Wilkes Booth. After shooting Lincoln in the head, Booth jumped onto the stage screaming, *"Sic semper tyrannis!** The South is avenged," breaking his leg in the process. Later, law enforcement officers caught and shot him and then hanged several of his associates. When Lincoln died, his secretary of war, Edwin M. Stanton, said at his deathbed, "Now he belongs to the ages."

What You Might Not: Conspiracy buffs of the day analyzed Lincoln's assassination just like today's conspiracists examine Kennedy's. Some even speculated that the mastermind was someone else, a man who craved not the presidency, but the (nonexistent, as it turned out) Lincoln family fortune. Yes, all conspiracy fingers were pointed at his eldest son, Robert A. Lincoln, who was also suspiciously present for a separate assassination, that of . . .

JAMES GARFIELD—JULY 2, 1881

What You Already Know: Somebody killed James Garfield.

What You Might Not: The assassin was Charles J. Guiteau, and besides being a bad person, he was an awful poet. Just before he was executed, Guiteau recited a hymn he'd written on the scaffold with the memorable (and perhaps excessively optimistic) title "I Am Going to the Lordy, I Am So Glad."

Also: Telephone inventor Alexander Graham Bell tried to find the bullet in Garfield with a metal detector, but failed due to the box springs in Garfield's bed.

Furthermore: Guiteau didn't *really* kill Garfield; Garfield's doctors did. For days, they probed the wound in his gut with

---

*   "Thus always to tyrants."

unclean instruments in search of the bullet; then they cut him open further to search for the bullet. The resulting infections and sepsis really caused Garfield's death. In fact, the bullet had lodged in a protective cyst, and, had they left the thing alone, he likely would have survived.

WILLIAM MCKINLEY—SEPTEMBER 6, 1901

What You Already Know: He was shot by an anarchist.

What You Might Not: That it's Leon Czolgosz, and it's pronounced CHOL-gaush. McKinley also died because his doctors couldn't find the bullet. As it happened, McKinley was shot at the Pan-American Exposition in Buffalo, New York. Oddly enough, a short distance from where he was attacked, an early X-ray machine was on display. Had anyone put two and two together, finding the bullet would have been a cinch. But no such luck; McKinley died after languishing in misery for several days.

JOHN F. KENNEDY—NOVEMBER 22, 1963

What You Already Know: Man, pretty much everything. That movie was, like, four hours long.

What You Might Not: According to biographer Seymour Hersh, Kennedy died not because he angered the Mafia or Cuban exiles or anyone other than Lee Harvey Oswald, but because of his debilitating back injuries. Kennedy, who often took narcotic pain medication for his back, was wearing an extra-rigid back brace for the Dallas trip, which made it impossible for him to duck the third (and fatal) shot. But all this talk of assassinations is making us depressed. C'mon, let's get a drink. . . .

06 Rounds From Around the World

PERU

Drink: pisco

Made from: grapes

Invented: by 16th-century Spanish conquistadors

Tastes like: smooth, sugary reeds

Cocktail: pisco sour

Hangover Factor: high, particularly at Andean altitudes

Fun Facts: Peru and Chile have a nasty, ongoing legal dispute over the rights to the "pisco" appellation. The name means "little bird" in Quechua.

BRAZIL

Drink: cachaça

Made from: sugarcane juice

Invented: accidentally, by Portuguese settlers, 16th century

Tastes like: rum

Cocktail: caipirinha, with sugar, crushed lime, and ice

Hangover Factor: high if you guzzle, but it's meant to be sipped slowly

Fun Facts: The settlers who inadvertently discovered it by letting their sugarcane juice ferment in the hot sun thought it was so awful they let their slaves have it all.

RURAL MEXICO

Drink: pulque

Made from: the sacred maguey plant

Invented: by ancient Mesoamericans

Tastes like: cheap Chardonnay mixed with apple cider

Cocktail: What are you, señor, a city boy?

Hangover Factor: low

Fun Facts: The Aztecs used it in religious ceremonies, along with those sacrifices. Like human blood, it doesn't keep, so make sure to drink it fresh.

CANADA

Drink: ice wine

Made from: naturally frozen grapes

Invented: by Germans

Tastes like: honey, candied fruit

Cocktail: Nah.

Hangover Factor: moderate to low

Fun Facts: Ice wine is hard to produce (or so its makers claim), so it's invariably overpriced.

FINLAND

Drink: Lappish hag's love potion (*lapin eukon lemmenjuoma*)

Made from: fermented blueberries

Invented: as far as anyone can tell, by a mythical Finnish crone

Tastes like: raspberries, oddly enough. It's red, too.

Cocktail: No, but there is a cocktail of the same name, usually made with blueberry syrup and vodka.

Hangover Factor: high. Drink it in the winter, so you don't have to face the sun.

Fun Facts: Those with respect for their elders prefer to call it "Lappish Grandmother's Love Potion."

CENTRAL ASIA

Drink: kumis

Invented: by Tartars, 13th century

Made from: fermented mare's milk

Tastes like: bile, by most accounts, but supposedly you get used to it

Cocktail: Probably almost any mixer could help.

Hangover Factor: extremely low. It's about 4 proof.

Fun Facts: Traditionally, it's made in a horsehide container called a *saba.*

COASTAL AFRICA

Drink: palm wine

Invented: lost in the mists of time

Made from: palm tree sap

Tastes like: candied dates

Cocktail: No.

Hangover Factor: low, but it's occasionally distilled extra long to create a sort of palm whiskey called arrack that should mess you up nicely

Fun Facts: so beloved, West Africans named an obscure, nearly extinct genre of guitar music after it: palm wine music

GREECE

Drink: ouzo

Invented: by Ottoman Turks. Descendant of Turkish liqueur called raki

Made from: grapes or raisins

Tastes like: anise

Cocktail: Hairy Armpit—one shot mixed with grapefruit juice over ice

Hangover Factor: moderate to high

Fun Facts: similar to the legendary French liqueur absinthe, minus the wormwood, the green fairies, and the inquisitive customs officers

NORTHERN EUROPE

Drink: mead

Invented: by benevolent Norse gods

Made From: honey and yeast

Tastes Like: honey

Cocktail: Mead Stinger, with bourbon and ice

Hangover Factor: low

Fun Facts: the original Anglo-Saxon wedding beverage, and probably the source of the word *honeymoon*. Which brings us nicely to . . .

07 The Seven-Year Itch:
Stories from the Annals of Divorce Court

JULIUS CAESAR VERSUS POMPEIA

Basically, this was ancient Rome's great ado about nothing. Pompeia, Caesar's pretty if somewhat dim political mismatch of a second bride, was designated to host the annual girls-only night known as Bona Dea. Unfortunately for her, a notorious beardless ne'er-do-well with the appropriately villainous name of Clodius Pulcher managed to crash the party disguised as a woman. He may well have been intending to seduce Pompeia, but his ruse was quickly discovered, and the poor girl probably didn't even know he was there till she heard about it from the gossips afterward. Nonetheless, her husband was prompt in declaring for posterity that complete innocence was beside the point, since "Caesar's wife must be beyond reproach," and that was it for her. Clodius was duly dragged off to court, but got off by bribing the jury. After the divorce, Pompeia predictably vanished from the history books and Caesar, after marrying one last time for appearances' sake, took off for the banks of the Nile and Cleopatra.

NAPOLÉON BONAPARTE VERSUS JOSÉPHINE DE BEAUHARNAIS

The tabloid celebrity split watch of their day from the very beginning, all of France was waiting for the inevitable. After all, it didn't take a Nostradamus to see it coming: His family despised her, and she cheated on him constantly. Yet the man was clearly smitten, and eventually she gave up infidelity, won over by his brilliant strategic barrage of sappy love letters from the front. The relationship lasted 13 years, only to prove conventional wisdom correct when it became clear she couldn't produce an heir. Still, it wasn't what you'd call an acrimonious break-up. From the transcript:

Napoléon: "She has adorned thirteen years of my life; the memory will always remain engraved on my heart."
Joséphine: "I am pleased to offer him the greatest proof of attachment and devotion ever offered on this earth."

After this sickening display, Napoléon went off to marry a teenager and lose Europe, and Josephine went off to die of a bad head cold. (Really.)

HENRY VIII VERSUS CATHERINE OF ARAGON

Technically an annulment—but one that neither the wife in question nor the pope ever recognized. In the breakup that started the Anglican Church, Henry VIII separated from Rome in no small part because he couldn't stand being married to Catherine. Of course, that was partly because she suffered from the gravest of all queenly sins—the inability to produce a male heir. After leaving Catherine, Henry went on to marry five more times. And though Cathy still considered herself married, she couldn't have thought much of her husband—especially since Henry sent her out to live in a series of dank prison castles. Although the rest of her life was miserable, Catherine won in the end. When her daughter, Mary, took the throne, her very first act was to annul the annulment. And speaking of royal rumbles . . .

08 King Me:
Outrageous Tales of European Royalty

Supposedly dour, English Queen Victoria's favored tipple in court was red wine spiked with a healthy dose of Scotch. This classy cocktail was allegedly invented especially for her by Scottish servant John Brown, with whom she may or may not have had a romantic relationship.

✳ ✳ ✳

Charles VI of France started out his reign, at the age of 12, with the promising *nom de roi* of "Charles the Well-Beloved." But by the time he'd hit his 20s, it was definitely "Charles the Mad." Charles wasn't wacky eccentric "Henry VIII" crazy or demented "George III" crazy. No, he was more of a dark, brooding, creepy, unpredictably enraged, "I wonder if the king's going to stab us in our sleep tonight" crazy. Eventually his council gave up trying to make him do any work on the pressing issues of the day, like the war with England, and just tried to stay out of his way. His wife, Isabeau, meanwhile, got to raise their 12 (!) kids while simultaneously negotiating treaties and caring for the affairs of state.

✳ ✳ ✳

Queen Juana ("La Loca"), on the other hand, was sadly unable to parlay her psychosis into a sweet life of leisure. Instead, she wound up locked in a windowless room for the last 32 years of her life. The sister of Catherine of Aragon and daughter of Ferdinand and Isabella, Juana was first driven to hysterical jealousy by her husband, Philip's, countless infidelities and then finally pushed into complete derangement by his death. As the only legitimate claimant to the throne of the dead Isabella, she was then politically exploited in turn by her father and her son, both of whom kept her safely locked up, which is just what her beloved husband was, in fact, planning to do when he died.

✼ ✼ ✼

It wouldn't be a party without Dracula. No, he didn't drink blood, but Vlad III's fondness for impalement as a solution to all life's problems has not been overstated. He probably also did nail two Turkish ambassadors' turbans to their heads when they refused to take them off. Still, he wasn't all bad. By all accounts, the crime rate in Walachia went way, way down during his reign. Probably the nicest Vlad story tells of the golden cup he set unguarded at a Walachian spring for travelers to drink from, which was never once stolen during his reign, because everyone was terrified of being gutted on a giant stake. Makes you feel all warm and fuzzy. In any case, he was generally regarded at the time, throughout so-called Christendom, as something of an unpleasant necessity, since he gleefully butchered so many prospective invaders. Speaking of invasions . . .

09 A Quick History of the Crusades

1095: First Crusade. Pope Urban II calls on all good Christians to come to the aid of the embattled Byzantine Empire and take back the Holy Land, since Europe is getting dirty and crowded, and the Middle East, as everyone knows, is nothing but milk and honey.

1098: Jerusalem is captured by the crusaders.

1145: Second Crusade. Edessa, an ancient city in the Holy Land, is retaken by Turks. The Vatican calls for a second Crusade, but Christendom is still tired from the last one and begs off. Eventually, Saint Bernard of Clairvaux guilts a few suckers into going.

1187: Saladin, having united the Muslims, recaptures

Jerusalem. Pope Gregory VIII, taking a new psychological tack, declares the recapture punishment for European sin. Feeling guilty, European Christians gear up for the Third Crusade.

1191: Richard the Lion-Hearted leads the crusader coalition to victory at the Battle of Acre. When Saladin refuses to meet treaty terms, Richard shows him who's boss by killing 5,000 helpless Muslim prisoners. Saladin still refuses to give up Jerusalem.

1198: Crusade Numero Four. Pope Innocent III calls for the recapture of Jerusalem. Instead of doing that, the crusaders, in 1204, somehow get it in their heads to attack Constantinople, even though it is technically a Christian city (albeit an Orthodox one).

1209: the Albigensian Crusade, which doesn't get a number because instead of Muslims, the pope's target was a bunch of vegetarian heretics in southern France called the Cathars. This operation is ultimately successful, since the Cathars don't have much of an army. Plus France is a much easier commute than previous Crusade targets.

1228: Sixth Crusade. Holy Roman Emperor Frederick II retakes most of Jerusalem, the first victory for Christiandom in several decades. It proves to be short-lived. . . .

1244: Muslims retake Jerusalem.

1248: Seventh Crusade. Louis IX of France undertakes an invasion of Egypt. He fails miserably, but somehow or other ends up becoming a Catholic saint, which is more than can be said for any of the seven French Louises who followed him.

1270: Eighth Crusade. Louis gives it another shot, this time attacking Tunis. His whole army falls sick from bad Tunisian drinking water, and Louis himself dies from a "stomach flux." His last word is "Jerusalem," which is not nearby.

1281: Ninth Crusade. The Venetians, apparently out of spite, decide to sack Constantinople again, but change their minds before arriving at the city. This proves to be the final crusade, at least until 1989, when Harrison Ford, with his rippling stomach muscles, finally finds the Holy Grail. And how'd he get those stomach muscles anyway? . . .

10 8-Minute Abs and Other Health Crazes

In 1997, the videotape fitness industry hit a home run with the informercial-sold fitness tape *:08min. Abs*. Simultaneously appealing to our desires to have rock-hard abs and our desire not to work very hard to get them, *:08min. Abs* promised you'd start to see results within a week and that you'd know the program worked because you'd "feel the burn." (It *does* work, by the way, at least in the sense of strengthening your stomach muscles, but it doesn't improve overall fitness much.) Only one problem: eight minutes is a *really* long time. Solution: In 1998, fitness expert Kurt Brungardt published the book *3-Minute Abs*.

Folk Medicine

Talk about your crazy health ideas. Here's a sampling of how Americans treated disease in the 19th century:

Whooping cough: Eat minnows (or, for the animal rights activists, just let them flop around in your mouth for a bit).

Cancer: Touch a dead man's hand to the affected area of the body.

Headache: Apply a sliced onion to your forehead (and weep out the pain).

Epilepsy: Ingest the afterbirth of a firstborn child. Or, if that doesn't suit your fancy, ingest blood—your family's blood is said to be particularly effective.

Measles: Drink sheep manure tea.

Tuberculosis: Drink cow manure tea (or ingest tree sap or eat molasses mixed with particles of iron).

Pimples: Give yourself a cow manure facial (careful, folks: Sources say that leaving fresh cow manure on your face for too long will turn your skin green).

Tooth decay: Stuff the cavities with cow manure. Or salt or spiderwebs. Or hen manure, for variety.

Charles Atlas is believed to have posed for the statue of George Washington in New York City's Washington Square Park, which explains why that particular likeness of Washington is so incredibly ripped. Speaking of great works of art . . .

✖ ✖ ✖

Former self-described "scrawny weakling" Charles Atlas became the most perfect physical specimen of manhood in the mid-20th century—or at least that's what the comic book advertisements said. Angelo Siciliano emigrated to New York from Italy as a child, and after getting pounded by Brooklyn bullies for a few years, he came up with the idea of muscle-against-muscle fitness training, now known as isometric exercise. He soon grew to be a huge hulking mass of mandom, got a job as a strongman in a Coney Island freak show, and changed his name to Charles Atlas. Atlas started his mail-order fitness business in 1928, and it's still around today (although admittedly, it's not the commercial juggernaut it once was). Atlas himself, however, is not. He died at 79, shortly after his daily jog—which just confirms what 97-pound weaklings like us have always thought of jogging.

8

01 Schoolhouse Rock!:
Art Schools We're Nuts About

RENAISSANCE

Period: 14th and 15th centuries in Italy, 16th century throughout Europe

Major Artists: your basic Ninja Turtles: Leonardo, Michelangelo, Donatello, and (to a lesser extent) Raphael

Hallmarks: true-to-life dimensions in sculpture; improved use of perspective

What It Depicts: biblical events or classical Greco-Roman scenes. Occasional Mona Lisas. And rich people.

TV Show It Calls to Mind: smart, pretty, and keenly rational . . . *CSI*

BAROQUE

Period: 17th century

Major Artists: Caravaggio, Rembrandt, Peter Paul Rubens

Hallmarks: deep, dramatic color, bright lights, and dark shadows

What It Depicts: saints, or the Virgin, or Jesus in moments of intense crisis. And rich people.

TV Show It Calls to Mind: uber-dramatic . . . *90210*

ROMANTICISM

Period: Late 18th–early 19th centuries

Major Artists: J.M.W. Turner, Delacroix, and Gericault

Hallmarks: sensuous color, slightly disjointed scenes—paving the way for Impressionism

What It Depicts: landscapes, everyday folks, war, liberty leading the people. And sometimes rich people.

TV Show It Calls to Mind: masterfully made, but almost embarrassingly sincere . . . *ER*

IMPRESSIONISM

Period: 1860ish–1910ish

Major Artists: Monet, Manet, Renoir, Degas

Hallmarks: visible brushstrokes, lighter colors—often said to look like something from a distance and nothing up close

What It Depicts: hayfields, lily pads, everyday people in everyday life, and naked people (Manet caused a scandal by painting nude people in contemporary settings). Fewer rich people.

TV Show It Calls to Mind: visually engaging and provocative, looks like something from a distance and nothing up close . . . *Twin Peaks*

DADA

Period: 1916–1924 (short, but important!)

Major Artists: Max Ernst, Marcel Duchamp, Beatrice Wood

Hallmarks: intentional absurdity, absolute meaninglessness, rejection of all assumptions about "art" and what constitutes it. World War I had messed people up pretty good, see.

What It Depicts: most famously, the pipe in Duchamp's painting *This is not a pipe.*

TV Show It Calls to Mind: endlessly ironic, self-conscious and vaguely sad despite all its humor . . . *The Simpsons*

CUBISM

Period: 1908ish–1920ish

Major Artists: Juan Gris and Marie Vassilieff, but Pablo Picasso dwarfed the others.

Hallmarks: Objects are taken apart and put back together again abstractly, skewing shape and perspective.

What It Depicts: women, guitars, violins

TV Show It Calls to Mind: some cutting-and-pasting segments on *Sesame Street*

ABSTRACT EXPRESSIONISM

Period: 1940s–1960s

Major Artists: Pollock, de Kooning, Rothko, Lee Krasner, Helen Frankenthaler

Hallmarks: massively abstracted images, spontaneity, unusual techniques (Pollock's drips and splatters, for instance)

What It Depicts: Heck if we know.

TV Show It Calls to Mind: Like, maybe if the color bars started dancing and fell in love with one another and revealed something about the subconscious? Of course, trying to define abstract expressionism in television terms is almost *criminal*, bringing us to . . .

02 Criminal Organizations Around the World

SICILY/AMERICA

Name: The Mafia (a.k.a. La Cosa Nostra, or "Our Thing")

Famous Faces: The five families are Bonanno, Colombo, Gambino, Genovese, and Lucchese.

Basics: Emerging out of Sicily in the mid-19th century, the Mafia spread to the U.S. East Coast in the early 20th century when a number of mafiosi fled there.

Fields of Operation: the protection racket, loan sharking, and old-fashioned grand theft

Current Level of Scariness: Still powerful in Sicily, but in America, the Sopranos make a lot more money than the Gambinos.

Media Saturation Level: extremely high. From brilliant movies like *The Godfather* to horrible movies like *The Godfather, Part III,* the Mafia's appealing mix of ethical conundrums and violent action scenes make it perfect for pop culture.

How to Say "Your little friend, he sleeps with the fishes": "Il tuo amico piccolo, dorme con i pesci."

JAPAN

Name: Yakuza

Famous Faces: Yoshio Kodama, who united several Yakuza in the 1950s; Hisayuki Machii, the Korean founder of Japan's "Voice of the East" gang

Basics: As Japanese feudalism changed in the 17th and 18th centuries, many Samurai found themselves without a job. They became roving protectors and/or criminals, which eventually morphed into gangs of Yakuza.

Fields of Operation: semilegal real estate companies, loan sharking, gambling

Current Level of Scariness: still kinda scary. For instance, when a Yakuza member's been naughty, he has to commit yu-bitsume—i.e., cut off his fingertip and give it to his master. (For this reason, studio executives considered adding a fifth finger to Bob the Builder's hand for the Japanese version of the eponymous cartoon, lest kids mistake Bob for a Yakuza member.)

Media Saturation Level: moderate. Although certainly no media juggernaut, like their Italian brethren, the Yakuza have inspired at least two good American movies—Ridley Scott's *Black Rain* and Sydney Pollack's *The Yakuza*—and some great Japanese ones (Kitano's *Fireworks* and *Sonatine*) as well.

How to Say "Your little friend, he sleeps with the fishes": "*Anata no tomodachi, osakana to tomoni nemuru.*"

COLOMBIA

Name: Cali Cartel

Famous Faces: Founded by Gilberto "The Chess Player" Rodríguez Orejuela and José Santacruz Londoño

Basics: Once described by the DEA as "the most sophisticated organized crime syndicate in history," the Cali cartel controlled some 80 percent of the cocaine imported into America in the 1970s and '80s.

Fields of Operation: cocaine. Occasionally, to mix things up, murder.

Current Level of Scariness: moderate. Most of the chief players from the cartel are in jail, but a series of warring "baby cartels" have sprung up in its place.

How to Say "Your little friend, he sleeps with the fishes": "*Tu amigo pequeño, él duerme con los peces.*"

Media Saturation Level: lowish. Pablo Escobar and his Medellín cartel got way more press. Really, Orejuela and Londoño should be just as famous as Escobar. Speaking of people who ought to be more famous . . .

03 Righting History's Wrongs:
People Who Should Be More Famous

Sure, there's a bad rock band named after him, but Serbian-American Nikola Tesla doesn't get nearly the credit he deserves. Tesla's discoveries made alternating current—the form of electricity much more reliable than direct current—possible, and both Thomas Edison and George Westinghouse repeatedly bought, or stole, Tesla's work. Edison and Westinghouse ended up with fortunes and Nobel Prizes, while Tesla ended up toiling in obscurity. In his later years, he started seeking messages from outer space and falling in quasi-romantic love with pigeons (really—see p. 119), but who can blame him? He was always denied his rightful place in history—although he is now featured on the 100 Serbian dinars bill. Last we checked, neither Edison nor Westinghouse had made it onto anybody's money.

✳ ✳ ✳

With a name like Philo T. Farnsworth and an invention like television, it's amazing he's not more famous. The son of a sharecropper, Farnsworth (1906–1971) was always fascinated by technology. He was only 14 when he conceived the basic idea for a television, and by the time he was 21, his contraption had transmitted its first image (a single straight line—like Pong, except more boring). Sadly, Farnsworth's unwavering beam of light, which presaged everything from *The OC* to Tivo, was the last great accomplishment of his life. He grew depressed and spent the last decades of his life in a drunken stupor. If only Philo had realized the power of his own invention: Who needs booze to treat depression when there's a *Laguna Beach* marathon on MTV?

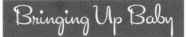

Bringing Up Baby

In 1946, former *Vogue* editor Marion Donovan invented the first reusable, leakproof plastic diaper. Like an awesome mix between Martha Stewart and MacGyver, Donovan built the prototype with nothing but her shower curtain and a sewing machine. Donovan then went on to invent the first disposable diaper in 1951. Sure, diapers now account for nearly 1 percent of landfill waste, but that's not Marion's fault.

✖ ✖ ✖

It's a crying shame when the discoverer of history's greatest miracle drug isn't even the world's most famous Felix. (That would, of course, be The Cat.) Felix Hoffmann (1868–1946) was a shy chemist who never married, had no children, and was never well known. But he discovered the first stable form of acetylsalicylic acid, now known as aspirin. Hoffmann's first test subject was his arthritic father, who pronounced the medication a success. It became the first reliable, non-narcotic pain medication—and, as a bonus, it can slow the progress of heart disease. This was great for people everywhere—except opium manufacturers, who, pushed out of the aches-and-pains racket, had to find a new market. Fortunately, that's why God made musicians. . . .

04 Music and Opiates

BILLIE HOLIDAY

Accomplishments: probably the greatest jazz singer of all time (sorry, Ella)

Drug of Choice: heroin (although she smoked marijuana from the age of 12 on)

Consequences: As if her life wasn't sad enough, Holiday served eight months in prison for heroin possession. She was also banned from singing in clubs for the last decade of her life. Heroin wrecked Billie's voice, and she died—at 44—with just 70 cents in the bank and $750 strapped to her leg.

HANK WILLIAMS

Accomplishments: made country music darker, more thoughtful, more fun to listen to, and inspired every country musician who came after him

Drug of Choice: alcohol and morphine

Other drug users with the name Hank Williams include Hank *Monday Night Football* Williams Jr. and Hank "Punk Rock Country Singer" Williams III.

Consequences: Williams started using morphine to treat his back pain caused by the birth defect spina bifida. Unfortunately, his drug use quickly spiraled out of control. Shortly after his last single, "I'll Never Get Out of This World Alive," was released, Williams died of a whiskey and morphine overdose at the tender age of 29.

JAMES TAYLOR

Accomplishments: Taylor's had platinum albums, won Grammys, and appeared on *The Simpsons*.

Drug of Choice: Oh, he had a friend, all right: heroin.

Consequences: Taylor was addicted to heroin off and on from the mid-'60s to 1985, and while he eventually recovered, you don't want to hear some of the stuff he was putting out in the early '80s.

MILES DAVIS

Accomplishments: Invented or participated in most of the important jazz movements of the '50s, '60s, and '70s, from bebop to cool jazz to fusion to free jazz.

Drug of Choice: heroin. Then cocaine. And sometimes both together.

Consequences: Davis kicked a four-year heroin habit in 1950 by locking himself in a room. But in the 1970s, he discovered cocaine, which wrecked his body. In the '80s, he started covering Cyndi Lauper songs. Clearly, the damage had been done.

But Wait There's More

Other musicians known to have used opiates include Boy George, Chet Baker, Paul Butterfield, John Cage, John Coltrane, Ray Charles, Eric Clapton, Stan Getz, Billy Idol, Joan Jett, John Lennon, Little Richard, Elvis Presley, Dee Dee Ramone, and Brian Wilson.

SID VICIOUS

Accomplishments: early London punk rocker who joined the Sex Pistols in 1977 and rocked hard even though he literally didn't know how to play his instrument (the bass)

Drug of Choice: heroin. And also anything else.

Consequences: An IV-drug user by the age of 17, Vicious (probably) killed his girlfriend, Nancy, in a heroin-induced haze. A few months later, Vicious overdosed, possibly intentionally, on heroin. He was dead at 21.

NERO

Accomplishments: noted Roman emperor (54–68 CE) and Christian persecutor

Drug of Choice: opium

Consequences: Nero didn't use opium himself; he used it on another. Many believe he poisoned his adoptive brother, Britannicus, to ensure he ascended to the throne. On the long list of unlikable Roman emperors, Nero has to be near the top. In fact, most biblical scholars believe that the mark of the Beast (666) referred to in the Book of Revelation is a numerical representation of Nero's name. And speaking of Revelation . . .

05 The End of the World:

Different People's Conceptions of the End-time

Whether it's two billion years from now, when the Sun will no longer provide enough heat to support life on earth, or two hours from now in a nuclear holocaust, life on earth will inevitably come to an end. All religious traditions grapple with this fact. Here's what they've come up with so far.

CHRISTIANITY

Things Get Bad: At least according to the Book of Revelation, things will be very bad indeed. Weeping, gnashing of teeth, rending of garments, blood in the streets, etc. All of this will occur during "the Tribulation."

And Then: the Second Coming of Christ, wherein Christ—to quote the Nicene Creed—"comes again in glory to judge the living and the dead."

Until: the Rapture, wherein all Christians (or at least good ones, depending on your particular denomination) are moved from earth directly to heaven with no dying or passing Go.

ISLAM

Things Get Bad: The Last Judgment in Islam is known as the Qiyamah. At a time of God's choosing—no one knows when—Jesus (yes, *that* Jesus) will come down from heaven, end all wars, and kill ad-Dajjal (Islam's equivalent to an Antichrist).

And Then: Each and every person who ever lived will be bodily resurrected and judged by God. Those found wanting will be sent to hell either temporarily or permanently; those who have been good and faithful go to heaven.

Until: No, that's it, actually. For the record, most Muslims do believe that some "People of the Book," that is, Christians and Jews, will also get to heaven.

JUDAISM

Things Get Bad: The end of days, or *acharit hayamim,* will be marked by conflict and tumult. When? Well, the Talmud states that the world will only last 6,000 years—so many Orthodox Jews believe the world as we've always known it will end in 2240 CE.

And Then: All of Israel's enemies will be defeated, the twice-destroyed Temple will be rebuilt, the dead will be resurrected, and the Jewish Messiah will become King of Israel.

Until: God intervenes in the Battle of Armageddon, saving the Jews, evil leaves the world, and earth becomes perfect. It's like that Belinda Carlisle song: "They say in heaven love comes first/We'll make heaven a place on earth."

BUDDHISM

Things Get Bad: According to the Buddhist holy scripture, the Tipitaka, we'll know the end of the world is coming when morality disappears and people start following the "10 Amoral Concepts." Those concepts? Theft, violence, murder, lying, evil speaking, adultery, idle talk, covetousness, greed, and perverted lust. Um, uh-oh.

And Then: Once morality disappears, things will degenerate into misery.

Until: A Buddha named Maitreya (known in English as the "future Buddha"), the successor to the Buddha we all know and love, will arrive on earth and begin teaching the pure Dharma.

HINDUISM

Things Get Bad: Most Hindus believe that we are currently living in *Kali Yuga,* the Iron Age, or age of darkness. Unfortunately for us, that means that evil is on the upswing. Eventually, Vishnu will become incarnate for the 10th and final time. By then, karma will have been completely turned on its head, with good people suffering needlessly and the evil rising to ranks of power.

And Then: Shiva, "the Destroyer," will dissolve the evil and corrupt universe. And then, because all things are cyclical, the universe will simultaneously be reborn.

Until: We start getting evil again and get ourselves into another age of darkness. Most Hindus are careful not to put an exact time frame on eschatological matters. If you do, you can end up looking awfully foolish. . . .

06 Not the End of the World:
People and Groups Who Falsely Predicted the End-time

CAN'T KEEP THOSE DAVIDIANS DOWN

In 1942, a Seventh-day Adventist named Victor Houteff broke away from the church with 11 followers and founded a "Davidian" branch of the church in Waco, Tex. Davidian. Branch. Waco. You see where this is going. But what a winding path the church took.

✳ ✳ ✳

After Houteff died, his wife prophesied that the world would end on April 22, 1959. In point of fact, about the most interesting event of April 22, 1959, was the Yankees' Whitey Ford striking out 15 Washington Senators en route to a 1–0 victory. Several hundred members of the Davidians left after the non-Apocalypse, but—remarkably—dozens remained faithful. In 1962, Benjamin Roden became the group's leader and proclaimed himself successor to not only Ms. Houteff, but also to King David, noted star of the Hebrew Bible. Roden's wife became the new Davidian (get it?) when she

Go Ahead, Drink the Kool-Aid.

By now, "Don't drink the Kool-Aid" is a well-known admonishment not to buy into collective wisdom. It derives from the 1978 Jonestown massacre, when 914 followers of Jim Jones, including 276 children, committed suicide. But here's the thing: No one at Jonestown drank Kool-Aid. They drank cyanide-laced grape *Flavor Aid,* a Kool-Aid competitor—but the poor, innocent Kool-Aid man has been taking the fall ever since.

took over the church. She quickly declared that in the Second Coming, Christ would assume the body of a woman.

✖ ✖ ✖

You'd think by now the group would have theological whiplash, and yet it stayed together until 1981, when Vernon Howell, who would later rename himself David Koresh, showed up. By the time the ATF raided the compound in 1993, the Branch Davidians had 130 members. While their numbers dwindled after the massacre, Davidianism is *still* alive: A few people still claim to follow Koresh's teachings.

Prominent (False) Prophets

HENRY ADAMS

Famous for: being the grandson and great-grandson of American presidents and writing the memoir *The Education of Henry Adams,* which Modern Library named the Best Nonfiction Book of the 20th century

Prophecy: In his old age, with the confidence of a man who would not live to be proved wrong, Adams declared the world as we know it would end in 1921.

What Happened Instead: Adams's world as *he* knew it ended in 1918.

LOUIS FARRAKHAN

Famous for: leading the Nation of Islam, organizing the Million Man March, believing in flying saucers

Prophecy: He said that the Gulf War—the first one—would be "The war of Armageddon, which is the final war."

What Happened Instead: It turned out not to be the final war—not even between those two countries in that particular place.

JAKOB BERNOULLI

Famous for: being the mathematician behind the "Bernoulli numbers"

Prophecy: Bernoulli predicted that a comet first seen in 1680 would soon return and slam into the Earth with *Deep Impact*-esque results.

What Happened Instead: The comet hasn't been seen since.

RONALD REAGAN

Famous for: being the 40th President; 1951's *Bedtime for Bonzo*

Prophecy: In 1971, Reagan said, "For the first time ever, everything is in place for the battle of Armageddon and the Second Coming of Christ."

What Happened Instead: The world went on, and Reagan got elected president, which was a boon for conservatism and also for jelly beans, Reagan's favorite snack. Mmm . . . jelly beans. . . .

07 Candy Is Dandy

The story of the jelly bean is of one of the great marriages in the whole history of candy.

The Jelly Pre-Bean: The jelly part of jelly beans was first created thousands of years ago in Turkey—when it arrived in the English-speaking world, they called it Turkish delight. Delicious, sure, but Turkish delight left a sticky residue on fingers.

The Bean Pre-Jelly: Jordan almond candy is a "candy" that tastes a lot like bitter almonds. The candies are often served at weddings to represent the bitter and the sweet, but in our experience, Jordan almonds are shorter on sweet than Mike Tyson's marriage to Robin Givens. However, Jordan almond candy does have an often pastel, semihard crust.

The Marriage: Sometime in the 19th century, the crust of Jordan almond candies and Turkish delight were joined together in blissful matrimony.

Mars

The Good: In the 1920s, Frank Mars (1883–1934) invented a series of candy bars, including Snickers, which he named after a family horse, and Mars, which he named after himself. Frank wanted to keep the company small, but his short-tempered, ambitious son Forrest made it a huge success, branching out into everything from M&M's to high-end pet food.

The Bad: Forrest was famous for his M&M-flinging temper tantrums.

The Exceedingly Weird: Forrest also made his employees taste-test every single one of their products—including the aforementioned pet food.

✖ ✖ ✖

Sylvester Graham (1794–1851) was a Presbyterian minister who saw the two greatest evils in life as "venereal excess" and alcohol consumption. His solution to lust and booze was simple: a vegetarian diet. To make vegetarianism more palatable, he invented graham crackers in 1829.

✖ ✖ ✖

Few titans of industry have been more widely loved than Milton Snavely Hershey (1857–1945), whose elementary school nicknames we can only imagine. After he made it big by manufacturing America's first tasty milk chocolate, he returned to his hometown of Derry Church, Pa., where he built a giant factory and a school for orphans. In thanks, the people of Pennsylvania set about naming every single solitary item in the state after him.

✖ ✖ ✖

Although today he is remembered primarily for Crunch bars, Henri Nestlé (1814–1890) was the first man to invent a safe baby formula. Sadly, he was inspired by experience: Five of his 13 siblings died during childhood.

Life Savers

Before electric refrigeration became widespread and affordable (around 1920), summer was a bad time for chocolate makers. Looking for nonmelty revenue streams in 1912, Ohio chocolate manufacturer Clarence Crane developed a hard peppermint candy that could withstand summer heat. To make his candy even more summer-friendly (and to differentiate them from traditional mints, which were square), Crane shaped his invention after the round life preservers that were gaining popularity at the time. Unfortunately, Crane hocked his idea soon after. Between 1913 and 1987, 33.4 billion Life Savers were sold. And like so many inventors before him, Crane never saw a penny of the profits. But the sad story of Clarence Crane doesn't end there. He had this son, see. . . .

08 The Poetry of Drowning:
Writers Who Literally Drowned Their Sorrows

Hart Crane never got along with his Life Savers–inventing father, Clarence. While Clarence was an industrialist, Hart was a sensitive and effeminate boy obsessed with language. Father and son did reconcile, though, shortly before Clarence's death in 1931. By then, Hart was a well-known and relatively successful poet whose influences included Walt Whitman and Edgar Allan Poe. But he was tired of being known as the third-best poet of his time (behind e.e. cummings and T. S. Eliot—maybe Hart would have fared better if he'd gone by H. H. Crane). A year after his father's death, he announced, "Goodbye, everybody," and then leapt from the deck of a cruise ship—at which point he could have used a lifesaver of the noncandy variety. Hart's body was never found.

❉ ❉ ❉

On July 8, 1822, having recently suffered the death of two children and his wife, Mary's, nervous breakdown, the Romantic poet Percy Bysshe Shelley went sailing in his schooner. (This was back in the days when poets could afford schooners.) The ship, which was never terribly seaworthy, sank amid a sudden storm. Although it seems likely to have been an accident, rumors have swirled ever since that Shelley's death was a suicide.

❉ ❉ ❉

The author of such classic have-to-read-in-college novels as *To the Lighthouse* and *Mrs. Dalloway*, Virginia Woolf struggled for decades with mental illness. After writing her husband, Leonard, a heartbreaking note that began, "I feel certain I am going mad again," Woolf filled her pockets with stones and drowned herself in the River Ouse in 1941.

✖ ✖ ✖

In 1972, confessional poet John Berryman *intended* to die of drowning when he jumped off the Washington Avenue Bridge in Minneapolis—but he misjudged the wind and died instead on the rocky shore.

Literary Demises

It should come as no surprise that many writers, being such clever and creative people, have found unusual ways of dying.

406 BCE: Greek playwright Euripides is mauled to death by a pack of dogs.

1593: Christopher Marlowe is killed in a bar fight.

1825–1855: All six children of Maria Branwell and Patrick Brontë—including writers Anne, Charlotte, and Emily—die of tuberculosis.

1849: Edgar Allan Poe dies of either alcoholism or rabies.

1914(ish): Ambrose Bierce disappears in Mexico while following Pancho Villa. He was probably shot by bandits, although—who knows—he could just be chilling in Cancun, soaking up the sun and enjoying his 164th birthday.

1941: Sherwood Anderson dies after accidentally swallowing a toothpick.

1980: French literary critic Roland Barthes steps out into the street and gets run over by a truck.

1983: Having apparently failed to learn from Anderson the abundant risks of placing non-food items in your mouth, Tennessee Williams chokes to death on a bottle cap. But enough about writers' endings. Let's talk about their beginnings . . .

09 Great First Sentences in Literature
(and When to Use Them)

Whenever James Joyce comes up in conversation, or whenever someone stately and/or plump enters a room:

"Stately plump Buck Mulligan came from the stairhead, bearing a bowl of lather on which a mirror and a razor lay crossed."

—James Joyce, *Ulysses*

✳ ✳ ✳

Whenever you find yourself in Faulkner's hometown of Oxford, Mississippi:

"Sitting beside the road, watching the wagon mount the hill toward her, Lena thinks, 'I have come from Alabama: a fur piece.'"

—William Faulkner, *Light in August*

✳ ✳ ✳

Whenever a situation arises requiring a sad, wistful comment (you got dumped; you were passed over for a promotion; your favorite NASCAR driver just missed the Chase for the Cup):

"Ships at a distance have every man's wish on board."

—Zora Neale Hurston, *Their Eyes Were Watching God*

✳ ✳ ✳

Whenever you are called upon to say anything about a family—yours or another:

"Happy families are all alike; every unhappy family is unhappy in its own way."

—Leo Tolstoy, *Anna Karenina*

✻ ✻ ✻

When introducing yourself to a curious stranger, or when the opportunity to take a jab at David Copperfield *arises:*

"If you really want to hear about it, the first thing you'll probably want to know is where I was born, and what my lousy childhood was like, and how my parents were occupied and all before they had me, and all that David Copperfield kind of crap,* but I don't feel like going into it, if you want to know the truth."

—J. D. Salinger, *The Catcher in the Rye*

✻ ✻ ✻

When you wish to simultaneously prove your intelligence and take a subtle jab at the patriarchy:

"Mrs. Dalloway said she would buy the flowers herself."

—Virginia Woolf, *Mrs. Dalloway*

✻ ✻ ✻

When you wish to convey your heartbrokenness or note how unrequited love smells a lot like arsenic:

"It was inevitable: the scent of bitter almonds always reminded him of the fate of unrequited love."

— Gabriel García Márquez, *Love in the Time of Cholera*

✻ ✻ ✻

When you're explaining that you've never read Ethan Frome *because the sheer number of commas in the first sentence scared you off:*

---

* That David Copperfield kind of crap: "Whether I shall turn out to be the hero of my own life, or whether that station will be held by anybody else, these pages must show." —Charles Dickens, *David Copperfield*

"I had the story, bit by bit, from various people, and, as generally happens in such cases, each time it was a different story."

—Edith Wharton, *Ethan Frome*

When you want to dispense advice of any variety, but you don't want to pretend it's your own advice because then no one would take you seriously, preface the advice with:

"In my younger and more vulnerable years my father gave me some advice that I've been turning over in my head ever since."

—F. Scott Fitzgerald, *The Great Gatsby*

✳ ✳ ✳

When you can't remember the other first sentences but you really want to quote the entire first sentence of a major 20th-century novel, we've found this one pretty easy to remember:

"Brrrrrrriiiiiiiiiiiiiiiiiiiinng!"

—Richard Wright, *Native Son*

(Note to perfectionists: It's one *B*, seven *r*'s, 19 *I*'s, 2 *n*'s, and 1 *g*. That kind of attention to detail will soon serve you well—you wouldn't want to drop a stitch. . . .

10 Rock, Paper, Scissors:
Arts and Crafts Around the World

PAPER

Origami, the art of folding paper, probably began around 105 CE, when the Chinese invented paper. "Hey," someone said, noticing, "you can fold this stuff in half!" But *origami* itself is a Japanese word, and it was in Japan that the art took on serious dimensions. Beginning in the 15th century, origami was used ceremonially—as elaborate gift wrap to folded-paper gifts for dead ancestors. These days, origami artists are capable of complicated creations. Although the rules of origami forbid cutting, pasting, or decorative touches, artists have managed to build everything from scale models of the Eiffel Tower to birds with flappable wings.

Known to Enjoy Origami: Spanish author Miguel de Unamuno, the Bauhaus design school (which taught origami as training for building design), and Friedrich Frobel, who invented kindergartens.

ROCK

If you really want your art to last, nothing beats rock (not even paper). The earliest known cave paintings are in France's Chauvet cave, or Grotte Chauvet (which is named for the guy who happened across it in 1994). Believed to be 32,000 years old, the cave's walls bear more than 300 paintings. Apparently, the ancient artists' favorite subject was, well, food—with the paintings at Chauvet depicting animals from owls to hyenas. In fact, much attention was paid to the craft, including the use of multiple colors. But while the French paintings have held up pretty well, the most sophisticated cave paintings are likely those found in Sub-Saharan Africa. There, painters used perspective, shading, and minute details to create realistic portraits of ancient animals.

Known to Be Rock Painters: Ancient folks on six continents! In the old days, rock was *the* canvas for aspiring artists everywhere.

SCISSORS

The first modern scrapbooks were called "commonplace books" and started showing up in the early 18th century. A luxury of the rich, commonplace books gathered together clipped newspaper articles, favorite quotations, small portraits, and locks of hair from friends. Oddly enough, among the most famous fans of commonplace books was Thomas Jefferson, and while there's no evidence he ever did so, we can't help but imagine Tom timidly asking Hancock, Washington, and Franklin if he might snip off a couple of locks for his special little book. These days, scrapbooks have played a key role, perhaps second only to knitting, in the crafting renaissance of the new millennium. No fewer than seven magazines currently cater to the scrapbooking market—including a bimonthly that employs the age-old trick of swapping *c* with *k* to cute-ify itself: *PaperKuts*.

Known to Be a Scrapbooker: The aforementioned Jefferson, Rutherford B. Hayes, and Mark Twain, who devoted many of his Sundays to scrapbooking and invented a self-pasting scrapbook. When he wasn't scrapbooking, Twain was busy being America's greatest comedian, as we'll soon see. . . .

g

🔲 All's Well:
The Original, Original Kings of Comedy

ARISTOPHANES

Overview: The inventor of comedy. The plot of his most famous play had the wives of dueling Athens and Sparta withhold sex from the warmongers until, finally, peace fell over the land.

Best Lines:

"Lopadotemachoselachogaleokranioleipsanodrimhypo-trimmatosilphioparaomelitokatakechymenokichlepikossy-phophattoperisteralektryonoptekephalliokigklopeleiola-goiosiraiobaphetraganopterygon." A grammatically correct Greek word that Aristophanes made up to poke fun at the Greek language.

"These impossible women . . . can't live with them, or without them!" Yeah—it's an old line.

SHAKESPEARE

Overview: Shakespearean humor generally falls under four categories: 1) horrible puns that rely on knowledge of 16th-century English; 2) veiled references to sex; 3) satire concerning

16th-century politics that scholars don't even laugh at; and 4) wit that, sometimes, remains timeless.

Best Lines:

"Though I am not naturally honest, I am so sometimes by chance."

"**Sampson:** . . . I will be cruel with the maids, I will cut off their heads.
 Gregory: The heads of the maids?
 Sampson: Ay, the heads of the maids, or their maidenheads; take it in what sense thou wilt."

MARK TWAIN

Overview: Mark Twain was the funniest writer in American history. We're going to stop the overview there to leave more room for his jokes.

Best Lines:

"I didn't attend the funeral, but I sent a nice letter saying that I approved of it."

"In a world without women," Twain was once asked, "what would men become?"

"Scarce, sir," Twain replied. "Mighty scarce."

"Familiarity breeds contempt—and children."

"It could probably be shown by facts and figures that there is no distinctly American criminal class except Congress."

LENNY BRUCE

Overview: Comedy's first bad boy, Bruce created the current form of stand-up storytelling with its sarcasm, twists, and shocks. In the '50s and '60s Bruce discussed topics ranging from his Jewish heritage to explicit sex and was arrested several times for public profanity—which does make him challenging to quote in a family-friendly book, but . . .

Best Lines:

"A lot of people say to me, 'Why did you [the Jews] kill Christ?' I dunno . . . it was one of those parties, got out of hand, you know? . . . We killed him because he didn't want to become a doctor, that's why we killed him."

RICHARD PRYOR

Overview: Born to a brothel's madam and one of her clients, Richard Pryor didn't get a head start in life. By making fun of himself, the state of the black race in America, and his own mistakes, Pryor became recognized as one of the finest comedians in American history. In the tradition of Lenny Bruce, not many of his best lines are suitable for publication. But we'll try.

Best Lines:

"I went to Zimbabwe . . . I know how white people feel in America now—relaxed! 'Cause when I heard the police car I knew they weren't coming after me!"

"I believe in the institution of marriage, and I intend to keep trying till I get it right."

Stricken with MS, Pryor stopped performing in the mid '90s, but he remained outspoken—but as an advocate for radical animal rights groups—until his death in 2005. Uh, we're guessing he wouldn't have liked what's coming . . .

02 Pets or Meat?

LOBSTERS

Loved as Pets by: French Romantic poet Gérard de Nerval, who kept his pet lobster on a leash during their frequent walks through Paris together

Devoured as Meat by: Everyone except vegetarians and Gérard de Nerval

Reasons to Love: De Nerval said, "They know the secrets of the sea, [and] they don't bark."

Reasons to Hate: ugly, unfriendly, clawed

Reasons to Eat: juicy, succulent, high-protein, low-fat deliciousness

Reasons to Abstain: It takes 45 minutes of shell cracking to uncover each tiny sliver of meat.

Verdict: PET!

EELS

Loved as Pets by: ancient Romans, who had an endless fascination with exotic creatures

Devoured as Meat by: anyone who can pronounce *unagi*

Reasons to Love: With no claws and no teeth, they can be played with all day long.

Reasons to Hate: Playing with an eel gets boring fast.

Reasons to Eat: 50,000,000 Japanese people can't be wrong.

Reasons to Abstain: In Günter Grass's novel *The Tin Drum,* Oskar's mother goes insane (and eventually dies) after seeing a severed horse head used as bait for eel fishing, leading Grass to write the classic line, ". . . for eel thou art, to eel returnest."

Verdict: insanity or no—MEAT!

SHARKS

Loved as Pets by: ostracized teenage malcontents

Devoured as Meat by: lots of people, apparently, since shark fin soup sometimes sells for $120 a bowl in Hong Kong

Reasons to Love: They're wise, ancient stewards of the sea.

Reasons to Hate: will eat you alive given half a chance

Reasons to Eat: We must prove to the sharks that *we're* on top of the food chain.

Reasons to Abstain: Fishing has decimated shark populations; if we aren't careful, kids 20 years from now will find *Jaws* about as scary as *Beak: The Killer Passenger Pigeon.*

Verdict: MEAT!

GOLDFISH

Loved as Pets by: seven-year-olds who won Goldy at a carnival game

Devoured as Meat by: drunk collegiate frat boys

Reasons to Love: 'cause Mom won't let you get a puppy

Reasons to Hate: dumb, useless, short life span

Reasons to Eat: Live sushi is *très chic.*

Reasons to Abstain: Goldfish crackers taste much better.

Verdict: PET! To anyone even vaguely normal, that is. But at frat parties, anything goes. Just ask . . . Bob Dylan?

03 *Greek Life:*
Surprising Fraternity/Sorority Members

BOB DYLAN — Back when he was Robert Zimmerman, Dylan belonged to a Jewish fraternity at the University of Minnesota—well, until he dropped out. Fans likely wish he'd stayed close to his Jewish roots—the three albums Dylan made during his stint as a born-again Christian are generally regarded to be among his worst. For what it's worth, though, Dylan didn't seem to think highly of his frat-boy experience. In a poem titled "Last Thoughts on Woody Guthrie," Dylan wrote, ". . . Hope's just a word . . . /But that's what you need, man, and you need it bad . . . /And it ain't in no fat kid's fraternity house. . . ."

✻ ✻ ✻

HARPER LEE — How could Ms. Lee ever have imagined such a charming and realistic social outcast as Boo Radley when she was an attractive and popular Chi Omega? Well, one of the more pervasive literary conspiracy theories in history is that Harper Lee didn't write *To Kill a Mockingbird* at all. It was, the conspirators say, none other than her friend Truman Capote (who, as a Southern homosexual, sure knew something about being an outcast). But like most conspiracy theories, this one doesn't hold up to close scrutiny—Capote was a versatile writer, but never composed anything with the tone or structure of *To Kill a Mockingbird*.

Fellow Chi Omega: Lucy Liu

✻ ✻ ✻

GEORGIA O'KEEFE — All we have to say about this is that the boys at UVA must have had a lot of panty raids at Kappa

Delta, Georgia's sorority, because those "flowers" she painted sure weren't wearing underwear.

Fellow Kappa Delta: 1983 Miss America Debra Sue Maffett (-Wilson)

✳ ✳ ✳

BILL COSBY — One of the oldest and largest black fraternities, Omega Psi Phi, claims Langston Hughes and Michael Jordan as members, along with the famously sweatered Huxtable patriarch.

✳ ✳ ✳

W.E.B. DU BOIS — Author of the classic *The Souls of Black Folk,* Du Bois was an early member of Alpha Phi Alpha, the first Greek-lettered fraternity for black college students, at Fisk University. Du Bois went on to get his PhD from Harvard, where fraternities have a very minor presence due to the prominence of "final clubs," which are exactly like fraternities except more pretentious.

JERRY SPRINGER — In the 1960s, Springer joined the Tau Epsilon Phi fraternity at Tulane. TEP is now defunct, although we can't say for sure whether they disbanded because they couldn't bear the humiliation of having Jerry Springer as their most famous member.

✳ ✳ ✳

BOB BARKER — It's hard to imagine the 273-year-old Bob Barker as a college student, but apparently he once was. And although he is a long way removed from his life as a member of Sigma Nu, Barker's *The Price Is Right* offers an excellent road-trip option for the latter-day *Animal House* residents among us.

✖ ✖ ✖

ORVILLE REDENBACHER — A member of a legal fraternity (Alpha Gamma Rho), it must have taken Redenbacher decades to put his rowdy frat days behind him (those legal fraternities party *hard*), because he didn't find success as a popcorn innovator until he was in his 60s. Redenbacher, incidentally, single-handedly created the subspecies of corn he bred for popability. As for some other great creators . . .

04 Creationists:
People Who Invented Their Genre

Thespis of Icaria created the one-man show while simultaneously creating the entire art form of acting when, in 534 or 535 BCE he jumped up onto his wooden cart and, instead of just telling a story, he pretended he was a character in the story. No one had ever thought to tell this particular kind of lie before, and it was a huge hit. Thespis became the most popular traveling bard in Greece, and the innovations of acting, costumes, masks, and makeup (all attributed to Thespis) spread throughout the empire.

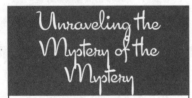

Unraveling the Mystery of the Mystery

At the top of a long list of writers widely suspected to have invented the detective novel are Agatha Christie and Sir Arthur Conan Doyle. However, the actual culprits were one Edgar Allan Poe, famous for explorations of death, and the now obscure (though once wildly popular) author, Wilkie Collins.

✖ ✖ ✖

Back in 1952, *Astro Boy* (*Tetsuwan Atomu* to the Japanese) first hit shelves of comic bookstores, officially launching the genre of robots, shiny boots, and large heads known collectively as Japanese animation or anime. The artist and writer behind *Astro Boy*, Osamu Tezuka, is known as the "god-king of *manga*," (*manga* being Japanese comic books) and the father of anime. In his lifetime, he drew over 170,000 pages of comics.

✖ ✖ ✖

While everyone knows Isaac Newton created classical mechanics, the system of laws governing physical bodies that's also known as Newtonian physics, not everyone is aware that the most influential scientist in history was also responsible for the cat flap. That's right! That little flap on your door that lets Kitty in and out without your having to lift a thumb comes straight from the mind of Sir Isaac. While the cat flap has lasted with relatively little change, Newtonian physics remained the only genre of physics for several hundred years, until Einstein, Planck, Bohr, Heisenberg, and a band of scientists proved that many of

Poe set the stage with three novels in which his hero, Auguste Dupin, follows convoluted trails to the truth using logic and astute observation. And while that proved a good start, the genre of detective fiction didn't truly emerge until Wilkie Collins introduced archetypes such as the inept police force, the celebrated private investigator, the reconstruction of the crime, and the final plot twist in his 1860 novel *The Woman in White*. The truth is Wilkie had mastered the genre over 15 years before the first Sherlock Holmes novel was even published.

Stealing Simba

Before his death in 1989, Tezuka said that the large-eyes style of Japanese drawing actually originated from American cartoons such as Walt Disney's Mickey Mouse. The trade of ideas runs both ways apparently, as Disney writers seem to have pulled many of the characters and situations in the movie *The Lion King* directly from Osamu Tezuka's *manga* (and full-length animated movie) *Kimba the White Lion*.

Newton's ideas were, well, a little off. Pretty soon the classical was replaced with the quantum. Quantum mechanics, incidentally, raises all kinds of interesting questions about . . .

05 Time Travel

Isaac Newton postulated that time was a constant everywhere and that, in essence, there was a clock somewhere by which everything was set. When Einstein published his theories of relativity, Newton's seemingly obvious arguments turned out to be entirely false. However, upon contradicting Sir Isaac Newton, Einstein wrote a very nice letter to the long-dead knighted nerd, which began, "Newton, forgive me."

✳ ✳ ✳

The worst thing about time travel is that it's so easy to do. You can move forward in time at the rate of one minute per minute for an infinite number of minutes. The real trick is traveling at a rate of two minutes per minute. Or, if we're interested in mounting a Tyrannosaur head on the wall of our study, we can get really

How to Build a Time Machine in Two Easy Steps

Step 1. Acquire an infinitely long, indestructible, and extremely dense cylinder. Okay, maybe the steps aren't so easy after all.

Step 2: Figure out a way to get your cylinder to spin amazingly fast. According to the theory of special relativity, a spaceship spiraling around the spinning cylinder could move forward or backward in time. Of course, the spaceship could not go back in time past the moment when the cylinder was built. Before that time, there no longer would be a time machine to carry the ship backward.

nutty and try to figure out how to go backward. Fast-forwarding through time, at least according to quantum mechanics, is entirely possible. All one need do is tool around the universe near the speed of light. Time would seem to pass normally for you, but to an outside observer you would seem to age extremely slowly.

TIME MACHINES THAT DON'T WORK:

slingshotting around the sun (William Shatner)

freezing your head (Baseball Hall of Famer Ted Williams)

the combination of internal combustion, a flux capacitor, and 1.21 jigowatts (Michael J. Fox)

Time Travel in Times Past

It didn't start with *Back to the Future*. We've been pretending to travel in time for as long as we realized there was time. Preagricultural peoples believed that time was not linear, but that everything happening has happened and will happen again. This cyclical nature of time allowed for communication to the past by sending messages into the future. And well before H. G. Wells kickstarted the time-travel genre with *The Time Machine*, Rip Van Winkle had already slept for decades.

✖ ✖ ✖

Speaking of which, the issue of Marty McFly's disappearing photo is a matter of considerable debate among physicists. What if you were to travel back in time and kill your virgin grandfather. Would you instantaneously disappear? And if you had never existed, how could you have killed your grandfather? Ow—contemplating these questions is giving us a stabbing pain in the head. Stabbing pains . . . stabbing pains . . .

06 Famous (Real) Duels

We tend to side with Mark Twain when it comes to duels. "I thoroughly disapprove of duels," he wrote in his *Autobiography*. "I consider them unwise, and I know they are dangerous. Also, sinful. If a man should challenge me, I would take him kindly and forgivingly by the hand and lead him to a quiet retired spot and kill him." Throughout history, however, others have lacked Twain's wisdom.

WILD BILL HICKOK VERSUS DAVIS TUTT

In the Red Corner: Wild Bill Hickok (1837–1876), legendary resident of the Wild West

In the Blue Corner: Davis Tutt. There's a reason you've never heard of him.

The Feud: On July 21, 1865, Tutt and Hickok settled a poker disagreement with the first known quick-draw duel in the American West.

The Fallout: Like we said, there's a reason you never heard of Tutt. He shot first and missed. Hickok shot second and didn't.

TYCHO BRAHE VERSUS MANDERUP PARSBJERG

In the Red Corner: Tycho Brahe (1546–1601), the Danish astronomer who coined the word *nova* and spent half his life living on an island observing the stars. His assistant, Johannes Kepler, later used Brahe's data to figure out planetary motion.

In the Blue Corner: some math nerd named Manderup Parsbjerg

The Feud: The two had an argument about mathematics. Honestly. Back then people didn't joke about numbers.

The Fallout: They dueled with swords in the dead of night, and Parsbjerg came up the winner. Brahe didn't die that night, but he did lose more than half his nose. For the rest of his life he wore a nasal prosthesis made of gold and silver.

ALEKSANDR PUSHKIN VERSUS GEORGES D'ANTHÈS

In the Red Corner: Aleksandr Pushkin (1799–1837), Russia's poet laureate, who wrote *The Bronze Horseman* and *Eugene Onegin.* Married to Natalya Goncharova.

In the Blue Corner: Georges d'Anthès, a Frenchman sleeping with Natalya Goncharova

The Feud: Pushkin tolerated gossip that his wife was having an affair with d'Anthès until he received an anonymous note nominating him to "The Society of Cuckolds." Already a veteran of several duels, Pushkin figured, hey, it's just a Frenchman.

The Fallout: D'Anthès shot first, mortally wounding Pushkin in the gut. Pushkin only managed to clip d'Anthès in the arm. Russia's finest poet was dead before his 40th birthday, while the thoroughly unremarkable d'Anthès lived to the age of 83.

ALI VERSUS FRAZIER

In the Red Corner: Muhammad Ali, the fast-talking, self-declared pretty, floating heavyweight

In the Blue Corner: Joe Frazier, the fierce, hard-punching heavyweight

The Feud: Their three fights (Ali won the last two) were

brilliant, epic duels. The feud, though, continues to this day. Frazier will not talk to Ali because he was so deeply hurt by Ali calling him a "gorilla."

The Fallout: Both men ended up with brain injuries as a result of their careers, but Ali is now considered the greater fighter (and person). Ali's prominence, in fact, eclipses more than just Frazier's. . . .

07 Lesser-Known Civil Rights Figures

JACK JOHNSON (1878–1946)

Overshadowed by: Muhammad Ali, Joe Frazier, Joe Louis, George Foreman

The Story: Jack Johnson had to chase white boxers all over the world to get them to fight him. In 1908, Johnson knocked out Tommy Burns in Sydney, Australia, and became the first African American heavyweight champion of the world. Over the next seven years he would defeat a series of Great White Hopes before losing to Jess Willard. Throughout his life, Johnson refused to live the life white people expected of him. He dated (and married) white women, drove fast cars, and dressed extravagantly. While he was champion, he was convicted unjustly of what amounted to white slavery (for transporting his own wife across state lines) and later served a year in jail on the charge.

LESTER MADDOX (1915–2003)

Overshadowed by: George "Segregation Today, Segregation Tomorrow, Segregation Forever" Wallace

The Story: Maddox was elected governor of Georgia in 1966 pretty much entirely because he defied the Civil Rights Act by refusing to serve African Americans at his Pickrick Restaurant. He eventually sold the Pickrick so that he wouldn't have to integrate it. Yet Maddox turned out to be a moderate (or as close to a moderate as Georgia had in those days). He appointed more blacks to state jobs than any of his predecessors, for instance. Strangest of all, Maddox took up comedy after his political career ended. His stand-up partner? An African American prisoner Maddox had pardoned during his governorship.

ELLA BAKER (1903–1986)

Overshadowed by: Stokely Carmichael

The Story: Ella Baker was 54 years old—hardly a student— in 1960, when she became the organizational force behind the Student Nonviolent Coordinating Committee (known as SNCC, pron. SNICK). SNCC became a leading arm of the civil rights movement, working with Martin Luther King's Southern Christian Leadership Conference to organize sit-ins and eat-ins and drink-water-at-water-fountain-ins and the like. Baker was also a driving force behind the Freedom Riders.

MARION BARRY (B. 1936)

Overshadowed by: his own crack cocaine abuse

The Story: Before he was shot by Islamic terrorists (1977), before he was elected mayor of Washington, D.C. (1978), and before he was videotaped buying and smoking crack cocaine (1980), Marion Barry was the first chairman of the aforementioned SNCC. Barry left his doctoral program in chemistry (chemistry, eh?) when the opportunity appeared and has spent the time since in politics. Despite several drug-related brushes with the law, Barry is still on the City Council in Washington, D.C. No doubt Barry knows the difference between baking powder and cocaine (by which we only mean he studied chemistry!). And soon, so will you. . . .

❚❚ How to Spot Real from Fake

DRUGS

Strategy 1: Put the substance in question near a drug dog. Lest you worry that police somewhere are getting their German shepherds addicted to methamphetamine so the pups can sniff it out of suitcases: Drug dogs learn to find drugs the same way Shamu learns to jump—Pavlovian training. Trainers begin by thrilling pups with a tug-of-war game with an odorless white towel. Then the trainer wraps drugs in the towel and hides it. The dog searches out its favorite toy, and when it finds the towel, it gets another game of tug-of-war. Over time, the dog comes to associate tug-of-war with the smell of the drug. Given a couple years of intense training, dogs can be trained to sniff out marijuana, heroin, cocaine, meth, and even prescription narcotics.

Strategy 2: Get out your chemistry set. Or, more specifically, your Porta-Pak narcotics kit. Although primarily used by law enforcement, chemical reagents that test whether a substance is actually an illegal drug are available to the public. Mostly either plastic pouches or old-fashioned glass tubes, the products feature chemicals that change color when in the presence of various drugs—they're as easy to use as, and somewhat scientifically similar to, home pregnancy tests. Tests are available for everything from ephedrine to mescaline. In fact, back in 2001, it was through exactly such a test that police officers in Rochester, N.Y., discovered that a large number of club kids who thought they were ingesting the designer drug MDMA, or ecstasy, were actually taking Remifemin, which treats symptoms of menopause.

DIAMONDS

Strategy 1: Find a nonessential pane of glass. If your so-called diamond cuts the glass, there's a fair chance you've located the real deal. Unfortunately, a lot of good fakes *also* cut glass. So for extra security you should probably move on to . . .

Strategy 2: Flip your stone upside down and place it over a newspaper. If, looking through the diamond, you can read the news, we regret to inform you that your diamond is fake. If, on the other hand, the newsprint is unreadable, you're approaching verifiable diamondity.

Strategy 3: Diamonds disperse heat near instantaneously; fakes generally don't. You can test the speed of heat dispersal in a stone using a lot of complicated sensors and a tiny heat source—or you can just breathe on it. Use your hottest breath to fog up the stone. If it stayed fogged for a couple seconds, you've got a fake. If it doesn't fog up, you're money.

Strategy 4: The surest way to check the authenticity of a diamond is to put it under ultraviolet light. If you do not have a black light of your own, we suggest going on Mr. Toad's Wild Ride at Walt Disney World's Magic Kingdom. There's plenty of UV light, and the ride isn't all that wild—which gives you plenty of time to examine your stone. Most diamonds glow blue under ultraviolet light (although strong fluorescence actually lowers the value of a diamond). Ninety-nine percent of fakes don't.

As for how to spot real great writers from fake ones, they've been fighting over that for centuries. . . .

09 Recent Feuds in Literature

AMIS VERSUS AMIS

The Rivals: Kingsley Amis, author of *Lucky Jim,* and his son, Martin Amis, author of *The Rachel Papers*

How It Started: Kingsley told the *Guardian,* "If I was reviewing Martin under a pseudonym, I would say he works too hard and it shows."

Highlights: After Kingsley died, Martin responded in book form with *Koba the Dread,* a biography of Stalin that doubles as a damning condemnation of his father's Communist sympathies. But one wonders why Martin was so hurt—his reviews are sometimes much worse than what his dad said of him. Author Tibor Fischer said that reading Amis's 2003 *Yellow Dog* was akin to "your favourite uncle being caught in a school playground, masturbating."

The Conclusion: Kingsley is still dead; Martin is still one of the most important writers in contemporary Britain.

GORE VIDAL VERSUS NORMAN MAILER

The Rivals: Gore Vidal, best known for historical fiction (*Lincoln: A Novel,* 1984), and Norman Mailer, best known for the World War II novel *The Naked and the Dead* (1948)

How It Started: Mailer and Vidal hated each other throughout the 1950s. But the feud first came to a boil in 1971 on *The Dick Cavett Show.*

Highlights: Before the taping started, Mailer head-butted Vidal, who responded with a punch to Mailer's (ample) gut. That may not seem like much of a fight, but we're talking about famous *novelists* here, not guests of *Jerry Springer*.

The Conclusion: Mailer is probably the more respected novelist these days. Perennially said to be on the short list for the Nobel Prize, Mailer may never win because of his rampant sexism. "I'm not a misogynist," he once said, not entirely jokingly. "I just believe all women should be kept in cages."

LILLIAN HELLMAN VERSUS MARY MCCARTHY

The Rivals: Lillian Hellman (1905–1984), famous for her plays (*Toys in the Attic*), her relationship with detective novelist Dashiell Hammett, and for hating Mary McCarthy, and Mary McCarthy (1912–1989), famous for her novel *The Group* and for hating Lillian Hellman

How It Started: Hellman made a dismissive comment about the American author John Dos Passos, which McCarthy found offensive. The root of their feud was political: McCarthy felt Hellman was a Stalinist; Hellman felt McCarthy was a jerk.

Highlights: On *The Dick Cavett Show* (where apparently all great literary feuds got aired), McCarthy said of Hellman, "Every word she writes is a lie, including 'and' and 'the.'" Hellman responded with a $2.25 million lawsuit, which dragged on for decades, until both Hellman and McCarthy were dead.

The Conclusion: Both are now best remembered not for their work but for their feud. However, Hellman's second-to-last play, *Pentimento,* is still highly regarded by critics. And speaking of second-to-lasts . . .

10 Second-to-Lasts

Although it's hard to imagine these days, there was a time in which one could simultaneously embrace Judaism and Islam—Islam saw itself, as Christianity did, as an extension of Abraham's religion, not a replacement for it. One such example from the early days of Islam was Safiyya bint Huyayy, who may hold a world record for number of *y*'s in a single name and who was Muhammad's second-to-last wife. Bint Huyayy was from a Jewish tribe and Muhammad likely married her to prevent her from being sold into slavery.

Spoiler Alert!

If somehow you've managed to escape reading *The Tempest* all these years and don't want to know how it ends, skip to the next page! Okay. Everyone's still here, we're guessing. So, at the end of *The Tempest,* the magician Prospero breaks his staff in two and throws his magic books into the sea. Some critics have seen Prospero's magic as a metaphor for the theater and his final abandonment of it as a kind of subtle retirement announcement from Shakespeare himself. But according to many scholars' chronologies, Shakespeare pulled his spells out of the sea and dried them off for one least hurrah: *The Tempest* proved to be his second-to-last play; *Henry VIII,* a lesser achievement to be sure, was the last he wrote alone.

✷ ✷ ✷

Ulysses was James Joyce's second-to-last book; the second-to-last sentence of its second-to-last chapter gives a nice sense of the challenge involved in reading it: "Going to dark bed there was a square round Sinbad the Sailor roc's auk's egg in the night of the bed of all the auks of the rocs of Darkinbad the Brightdayler." (Having looked pretty closely at the annotations, we believe we can roughly translate that sentence: "Bloom went to bed.")

Second-to-Lasts, Briefly

Full Metal Jacket was Stanley Kubrick's second-to-last r

Joe DiMaggio was Marilyn Monroe's second-to-last band.

"Llewelyn the Last," who ruled Wales from 1258 to 1282 C was actually the second-to-last King of Wales.

Pope Benedict XVI is the second-to-last pope before the Second Coming, according to the 12th century prophecies of Saint Malachi.

Back when he was known as Eric Blair, George Orwell graduated second-to-last in his class at Britain's prestigious Eton public school. (When the Brits say "public school," they mean "private school.")

Despite rumors to the contrary, Ulysses S. Grant did *not* finish either second-to-last or last in his class at West Point. He finished 21st in his class of 39.

The Pot o' Gold was the second-to-last Lucky Charms marshmallow to be introduced (it showed up in 1994).

The second-to-last book of the Christian Bible is The Letter of Jude.

Frank Lloyd Wright's second-to-last building was a house built for physician Don Stromquist in Bountiful, Utah.

The second-to-last prime number to have been discovered was 2 to the 24036583 power—1. Containing 7,235,733 digits, it was discovered in 2004 by John Findlay (or, more properly, by his computer).

The second-to-last Spinal Tap drummer was Peter "James" Bond, who blew up in a (presumably hairspray-fueled) fire. Speaking of *Spinal Tap* drummers . . .

Ends Well:
Happy Endings

Maybe it's not a happy ending, but it's a funny one: Our favorite death in cinema comes courtesy of *Spinal Tap*, in which drummer Eric "Stumpy Joe" Childs chokes to death on someone else's vomit.

✖ ✖ ✖

It's estimated to have killed more than a hundred million people over the centuries, but smallpox is history—at least for now. That's because effective and harmless inoculations have existed for smallpox ever since Dr. Edward Jenner discovered, in 1796, that a milder disease, cowpox, worked as a smallpox vaccine. But as late as 1958, two million people were dying of smallpox every year. Beginning in 1967, teams of doctors worked to eliminate the disease by inoculating everyone near

The Happy Ending Problem

Our very favorite Happy Ending comes from the world of math. In 1933, a young Hungarian mathematician named George Szekeres was hanging out with his friends, chatting math, when a young woman named Esther Klein posed a problem: "Given five points in the plane in general position, prove that four of them form a convex quadrilateral." (Note: You don't have to understand that sentence to enjoy the story. We certainly don't.) George couldn't figure it out. But when Esther showed him her proof, they began discussing it, fell in love, and lived happily ever after. Ever since, the problem has been known in mathematics as "the Happy Ending problem." George and Esther were married for 68 years. They died a few hours apart on August 28, 2005.

an outbreak. The results worked. In 1977, smallpox became the first disease ever to be eradicated by human ingenuity.

RIP: AND, FINALLY, SOME GREAT LAST LINES AND WHEN TO USE THEM

When the topic is any form of history:

"If history has taught us anything, it is that you can kill anyone."

—*The Godfather: Part II*

✖ ✖ ✖

When being dragged away to a mental institution:

"I have always depended on the kindness of strangers."

—*A Streetcar Named Desire*

✖ ✖ ✖

To impress sci-fi nerds:

"If any of my circuits or gears will help, I'll gladly donate them."

—*Star Wars (Episode IV)*

✖ ✖ ✖

When you want to quote the last line movie buffs seem to enjoy the most:

"All right, Mr. DeMille. I'm ready for my close-up."

—*Sunset Boulevard*

✖ ✖ ✖

When you're trying to prove that 1933's King Kong *is a surprisingly intellectual and sophisticated movie:*

"Oh, no, it wasn't the airplanes. It was Beauty killed the Beast."

—*King Kong*

✖ ✖ ✖

You've just done something really good, and as a result of it, you're gonna die:

"It is a far, far better thing that I do, than I have ever done; it is a far, far better rest I go to than I have ever known."

—*A Tale of Two Cities*

✖ ✖ ✖

Someone tells you they didn't like a book you wrote that contained a lot of charmingly presented facts and figures and observations tenuously connected to one another:

"Well, nobody's perfect."

—*Some Like It Hot*

✖ ✖ ✖

Someone tells you they did like your book, and wouldn't it be nice if you wrote one about the differences between oft-confused nouns, like Monet and Manet.

"That might be the subject of a new story, but our present story is ended."

—*Crime and Punishment*

ABOUT THE EDITORS

Will Pearson and **Mangesh Hattikudur** met as freshmen at Duke University, and in their senior year parlayed their cafeteria conversations into the first issue of **mental_floss** magazine. Five years later, they're well on their way to creating a knowledge empire. In addition to the magazine, a board game, and a weekly CNN *Headline News* segment, the two have collaborated on five **mental_floss** books. Will and Mangesh also codirected *Citizen Kane* in 1941 while hiding inside a rubber Orson Welles suit.

✳ ✳ ✳

John Green is the author of the award-winning novel *Looking for Alaska* (2005), which has been translated into nine languages and is being made into a film by Paramount Pictures. John also contributes commentary to NPR's *All Things Considered* and works for *Booklist* magazine, reviewing literary fiction and children's picture books as well as pretty much everything that gets published involving boxing, conjoined twins, and/or little people (although John himself is quite tall). In short, his brain is pretty scattered.

ABOUT THE CONTRIBUTORS

Ransom Riggs is an award-winning film director and lives in Los Angeles—but despite that is a pretty nice guy. Before earning an MFA from the University of Southern California's renowned film school, he worked as a journalist, a photographer, and an editor of documentaries. You can find him on the Web at www.SpaceboyMovie.com.

✖ ✖ ✖

Will Hickman is a reclusive freelance writer living somewhere in Indiana. He is working on a book about college basketball, American politics, and the apocalypse.

✖ ✖ ✖

Hank Green lives in Missoula, Montana, where he works in front of a computer. He also plays, eats, writes, reads, and sometimes sleeps in front of a computer. Come to think of it, he doesn't really even stand up very often anymore. Most of the time he's a consultant for progressive campaigns, but occasionally he's Lieutenant Mike Powell, available on short notice for deadly, covert missions in Nazi Germany.

A Genius for Every Occasion . . .

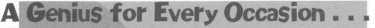

mental_floss Cocktail Party Cheat Sheets
0-06-088251-4 (paperback)
Available 6/06

Don't be a wallflower at your next social outing, just fake your way through the conversation! These cheat sheets will have you equipped to handle the brainiest of topics in no time.

mental_floss Scatterbrained
0-06-088250-6 (paperback)
Available 7/06

Based on *mental_floss* magazine's popular "Scatterbrained" section, this book features thousands of juicy facts and tantalizing bits of trivia that are connected humorously—from Greece (the country) to *Grease* (the movie) to greasy foods and on and on.

mental_floss What's the Difference?
0-06-088249-2 (paperback)
Available 7/06

Want to spot a Monet from a Manet, kung fu from karate, or Venus from Serena Williams? Piece of cake! Whether you're trying to impress your boss, mother-in-law, attractive singles, or your 4th grade teacher, *mental_floss* has hundreds of quick tricks to make you sound like a genius.

mental_floss Genius Instruction Manual
0-06-088253-0 (paperback)
Available 11/06

The *Genius Instruction Manual* is the ultimate crash course on how to talk, act, and even dress like a genius. Presented by the brainiac team at *mental_floss*, it's the one-stop shop for today's impossibly clever, cultured, and sophisticated person.

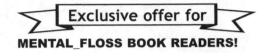

© Thomas Balsamo

Autism is heartbreaking.
But it's not hopeless.

Most people take smiling, talking and laughing for granted - simply part of being human. But for the more than one million Americans affected by autism, these simple human experiences are extremely difficult or nonexistent.

Autism is a neuro-developmental disorder that impairs, often severely, an individual's ability to communicate and interact with others. This impairment creates a world of isolation and frustration for even the sweetest and smartest of souls. Autism is painful and heartbreaking, but it's not hopeless.

At Cure Autism Now, we're accelerating scientific research to treat and cure autism. We believe in urgency, excellence in science, collaboration and open access to information. To learn more about our innovative research programs and how you can help, call us or visit us online.

cure
Autism
now
FOUNDATION

888.8.AUTISM
www.cureautismnow.org